CW01262183

Fire McGuire

A Novel by

Steve McElhenny

Copyright © 2024 Steve McElhenny

All rights reserved.

ISBN 9798324396398

DEDICATION

This book is dedicated to my ladies, Sian, Sophia, and Carys.

Fire McGuire – Steve McElhenny

"It's time to play the game."

The Game – **Motorhead**

Part One

Playing the Game

Scene One
Barry McGuire

If there was ever to be a category in the Guinness Book of World Records for, **Person Fired from the Highest Number of Jobs**, then standing at the summit of this dubious list, you would find the name of Barry McGuire - aged twenty-six, and residing in the small, Southern-English town of Chelmsley Green.

In the past nine months alone, McGuire had been fired from no less than thirteen different jobs – all of which had been upon the very first day of his fleeting employment.

In a town as small as Chelmsley Green, it was inevitable that the conversations amongst the locals would regularly veer from such cliched and uninspired small talk of subjects such as the weather, politics, or the previous night's television, towards that of McGuire's erroneous exploits. It was during one of these conversations that his moniker, Fire McGuire, had been birthed.

The speculation was rife amongst them as to why this charming, intelligent, and seemingly sane young man, came to be the recipient of so many sackings.

Often in life, however, the answers to the most challenging of questions are those which prove to be the simplest. For McGuire, getting fired from as many jobs as possible was merely a game to him - and one in which he found no greater pleasure than playing.

Like all games though, there must be rules. And as such, he had devised and imposed a strict set by which he had to abide. If he were to break any of these rules, he had bestowed upon himself, it would result in an instant disqualification and would prohibit him from playing his game ever again.

Rule One

No physical violence.

This was one of the most important commandments within his self-written rulebook. Under no circumstances was he ever to resort to any physical violence in order to get fired from a job. Not only was physically striking an employer, colleague, or even a customer, a potentially criminal and mentally scarring act but it was also a cheap and easy way out. McGuire saw himself as an artist, not a thug. He was a Van Gogh, not a Van Damme.

Even on the few occasions where McGuire's actions had seen his employer throw a fist at him in frustration or anger, he refused to fight back. It was an occupational hazard for his chosen pastime.

Rule Two
Never do anything that would cause the employer to go out of business.

As much as McGuire enjoyed the anarchy, chaos, and unpredictability of his game, he was still more than aware of the repercussions of his actions - should he ever take things too far.

Despite the limits he would push himself, and very often his employers to, it was still his responsibility to ensure no one's livelihood would be affected by his exploits. He may have been an asshole for much of the time, but he wasn't a monster.

Rule Three
No destruction of property.

Although there would, on occasion, be the inevitability of minor collateral damage, there was to be no vandalism of any property or equipment on his part which would cost the employer any significant amount of money to repair or replace.

Rule Four
No Walking Out.

The only way he would be allowed to leave a job was by being fired. If he had to quit, the sacking's not legit, and he would deem himself to be disqualified from playing his game.

Rule Five
Accept every job that's offered to you.

No matter what the job, if offered to him, he had to take it. It didn't matter if it was a dream job or the most menial one he could envisage, he couldn't show any favouritism in what jobs he would get fired from. Whereas most companies see themselves as equal-opportunity employers, McGuire saw himself as an equal-opportunity ex-employee. It didn't matter if it was a six-figure salary or a minimum wage position, all that was important was that before the end of the shift, he'd have been unceremoniously given his marching orders.

Rule Six
Never make things personal.

Though McGuire was frequently crass, inappropriate, and impertinent during his game, he vowed never to make any personal insults or comments to colleagues or customers that would cause them any undue misery. This specifically included comments about race, appearance, and creed. There was also a ban on any comments that could be construed as direct sexual harassment. After all, they were just innocent pawns in his game. More importantly, they were human beings, and any lowly taunting in this manner was just cruel, loathsome, and uncalled for.

Rule Seven

Don't be a Sicko.

Never take the easy way out by simply pulling a sicky for an unrealistic level of time - that's just a lazy and uninspired way of doing things. You may as well just quit if you're going to go on the sick until you're let go (See rule four). Getting fired by default is the same as filling out a puzzle in a crossword book by looking to the back pages for every single answer. Or searching for online spoilers to find the identity of a killer in a mystery story before you watch or read it. There's no thrill or challenge there, it just becomes an exercise in going through the motions.

Rule Eight
Never tell anyone about your game - ever.

No explanation required.

These eight simple rules were the only statutes McGuire confined himself to. Anything else, as far as he was concerned, was fair game in the workplace-sized gladiatorial arena of his unusual quest to get dismissed from as many occupations as possible.

With each sacking that occurred over the three years since beginning this game, however, McGuire was finding it increasingly harder to play.

Such was his reputation in Chelmsley Green and its surrounding towns and villages, any employment in these areas was now out of the question.

Also, with each new firing came with it yet another lousy reference for prospective employers to check upon - fervently warning them against hiring this trainwreck of a person named Barry McGuire.

He had already found himself blacklisted from many of the larger corporations, and on occasion, had even found it necessary to conjure up a variety of false documents and identities to get himself jobs and interviews.

It would be fair to say, McGuire worked very hard at not having to work at all. Aside from the diminishing number of career opportunities available for him to get fired from, he was also finding himself a new adversary in the form of Human Resources.

Contrary to popular belief, getting fired from some companies is a harder task than you may envisage. In a corporate world shackled by laborious legislations such as verbal warnings, written warnings, informal warnings, formal warnings, first warnings, final warnings, and first informal verbal warnings of a final formal written warning, McGuire sometimes had to go above and beyond to bypass them all and go straight to the instant dismissal.

Despite these growing obstacles, this year so far was proving to be particularly prolific for him. It was now Autumn, and by his calculations, he was well on track to beat his personal best for, Most-Sackings-in-a Single Calendar Year. His previous record had been fourteen. All he needed was two more dismissals in the next three months.

As he found himself being summoned to the office of his current employer, all the signs were looking likely that there would soon be another firing to his name.

Scene Two
Pet Hates

The hour hadn't even reached noon when McGuire heard his name being bellowed ominously.

The agitated tone demanding he immediately make his way to the office came from Julian Granger, the manager and proprietor, of the small pet and garden store - Pet Names.

The frayed emotion evident in Mr Granger's tone as he yelled was a good indication that McGuire was not being summoned for a positive appraisal for his first few hours of employment as a store assistant.

'Barry, come in and sit down please,' Mr Granger's wavering voice requested as he saw his employee coyly open the door after an equally delicate knock.

There was, of course, nothing coy or delicate about McGuire. His gentle demeanour was all part of his charade. He was the proverbial baby-faced assassin. Only this was no target he was intending to terminate, but his own employment.

As requested, he entered the homely-looking office and pulled up a chair opposite the flush-faced Mr Granger at his desk.

Framed pictures of Granger's family were positioned neatly on the desktop. Scattered less uniformly was a collection of barely legible drawings from whom McGuire could only assume were his young grandchildren. Either that or Mr Granger was incredibly shit at art.

In the almost three hours, he had known his middle-aged employer, he could already tell that Granger was a decent and morally-sound man - albeit one who was overly sensitive. He had a sense that this was why and how he had found himself to be in this business - a longing to do his part by dealing in products and advice that would help nurture and protect things that would flourish, grow, and bring happiness to their owners.

Had McGuire been more benevolent when playing his game, he would have taken Mr Granger's kindly and delicate disposition into account by being gentler with him as he prepared for the dismissal that was surely forthcoming. As it was, McGuire had decreed to himself that sentiment in situations such as these was an unnecessary burden. Whether the employer was a sonofabitch or the salt of the earth, they were still the same unwitting pawns in his game.

'You called for me, boss?' McGuire enquired with a well-rehearsed tone of innocence, despite knowing exactly why he had been called - After all, he had spent almost a week before his first day of work planning it.

Mr Granger couldn't bring himself to look his employee in the eyes. If he did, McGuire was certain his boss would break down in tears. Instead, he just reached for a poster that was noticeable upon his desk next to the other drawings. Unlike the other pictures, however, McGuire doubted very much this would ever be displayed proudly upon Mr Granger's fridge or wall.

'Do you care to explain this?' the manager asked.

'It's a poster,' the unassuming response came.

'I know it's a poster, Barry.' His voice was already close to breaking due to the strenuous cocktail of anger and distress. 'What I mean is, do you care to explain it?'

'Sure!' McGuire heartily enthused. 'It's an idea I had to increase business for this place. It's an advert for the rematch between the tortoise and the hare for later on today. Well, technically it's going to be a rabbit, but I think we can allow ourselves some artistic license in this case.'

'The tortoise and the hare was a race, Barry. The animals in this poster have weapons attached to them.'

To reiterate his point, Granger pointed at the offending poster where a photo of a young bunny rabbit had, photo-shopped onto its back, a blood-stained power drill attached to a harness. It was face to face with a tortoise, which had some crude explosives attached to its shell. The text on the poster in large, bold, red font, read.

> The Rematch of the Century
> The Tortoise and the Hare 2
> Pet shop Death Match
> Two Animals Enter
> One Will Leave…. In Pieces.

'This is madness,' Mr Granger decried. 'Do you know how many complaints I've already had today from parents of traumatised kids? I've spent almost the entire morning on the telephone apologising for this abomination of a poster.'

'Don't you think you're overreacting boss?' McGuire countered with a well-disguised mock blamelessness. 'I mean, granted, maybe one or two people may not appreciate an animal deathmatch taking place inside a pet shop, but believe me, I've had a lot of people tell me they're very interested too. The local newspaper seemed to be taking a particular interest when I phoned them up and told them about it.'

McGuire, of course, had not phoned any newspaper. That would have been a clear violation of Rule Number 2: Never do anything that would cause someone to go out of business. The multitude of complaints Mr Granger received, unbeknownst to him, had not even been from any members of the public. They had all been from McGuire on his mobile phone during his numerous visits to the stockroom. Thankfully, for McGuire, his besieged supervisor was too upset to question why so many of the locals of this small town had such an array of regional accents.

The truth was, no one other than Mr Granger and he had even seen the poster. The malignant employee placed it on the notice board of the store as and when he was sure only his manager would find it.

Upon hearing the revelation that the newspapers were now involved in this scandal, and with the mental image of derogatory headlines plastered over the pages flashing through his mind, Mr Granger found any restraint he still clung onto corrode away.

'Get out,' his voice thundered. Gone now was any trace of the store manager's meekness. This was primal rage. 'I never want to see your face again. You're fired, you hear me?'

McGuire did indeed hear him, and most likely, so did anyone within a fifty-metre radius.

If McGuire had ever professed himself to be a righteous man, he could have laid claim that this whole charade was done to benefit Mr Granger - an elaborate ruse to make him more of an assertive, stronger-spirited person. Yet, any personal growth was really of no consequence to him. All that was important to Barry was that he had just claimed another sacking to his name. He had equalled his personal best, and now he only needed one more firing before the end of the year to beat it.

Surely, he could not fail.

Pet Names Proudly Present

THE REMATCH OF THE CENTURY

THE TORTOISE AND THE HARE 2

PET SHOP DEATH MATCH

TWO ANIMALS ENTER
ONE WILL LEAVE.... IN PIECES

In Store September 28th

Scene Three
Interview with a Scamp Hire

Getting fired from as many jobs as he could was only one element of McGuire's game. There was just as much anarchic amusement to be found in attempting to gain employment in the first place.

McGuire had been called many things throughout the past several years, many of them unflattering - and even he would have to admit it was difficult to deny their accuracy. One thing he had yet to be correctly called by anyone, however, was a realist.

McGuire was confident enough in his impish abilities to blag his way through most situations, but even he was loathe to admit there were just some jobs that not even he could worm his way into. This still didn't stop him from applying for them, however - and sometimes, he would even get invited to the interview stage. After all, even a blind man throwing darts at a dartboard for long enough will hit a bullseye eventually.

On these occasions, he knew he was simply there to make up the numbers, and for interviews such as these, he saw it as an opportunity to really have some fun. Even if he held no realistic chance of landing a job offer from it, he would most certainly make it his edict to leave a lasting impression.

Over the three years since he had been playing his game, he had developed a substantial list of techniques to ensure he would leave a lasting impression. The following are just a handful of examples he had perfected.

Technique One
Don't be afraid to ask for help.

This technique is one McGuire had honed into a fine art and

was guaranteed to throw any job interview into an unappetising cocktail of chaos and confusion, with an added garnish of exasperation.

The interview would start innocuously enough, and without any indication of the impending disarray. McGuire would even strive to remain as bland and as unimpressionable as possible.

With the banal formalities of introductions and small talk over - and having lulled his unsuspecting interrogators into a false sense of superiority - it would be time for him to sow the first few seeds of disorder.

Job interviewers are often a predictable sort, and their insipid questions even more so. They almost always contain the same well-worn line of cliched questioning. 'Why do you want this job? What do you think you can bring to this role? What are your long-term goals?'

It would be at this point McGuire would sit there in silence with a dumbfounded expression for an uncomfortably prolonged period of time before subtly, yet noticeably, pulling out a mobile phone from his pocket. He would then twist his body around enough to be facing away from the interviewer, before pressing a couple of buttons and begin to speak into the phone.

'Jeff,' he would whisper loud enough to ensure anyone else in the room would be able to hear. 'It's Barry. I'm at that job interview and they just asked me what I can bring to this role. I haven't got a clue what I could bring. What the hell do I say?'

After several moments of a lingering and surreal silence, McGuire would nonchalantly turn around as if nothing other than the status quo had just happened and confidently reel off an answer he had clearly just been fed.

There was, of course, no one on the other end of the phone. Yet, the interviewers weren't aware of this - and even if they had been, it only added to their befuddlement.

'Er, did you just phone someone Mr McGuire?' the disbelieving riposte would often come.

'No,' he would reply in a tone that suggested he was offended by such an outrageous allegation.
The next question would then come. Only, inevitably, it would be delivered with far less authority and confidence than its predecessor. Again, McGuire would look dumbfounded before pulling out the phone, turning away, and asking for guidance once more. After about half a baffling minute, he would then turn back around and rattle off yet another, perfect, paraphrased answer. Only, this time, he wouldn't even bother putting his phone back in his pocket.

'You did it again, Mr McGuire. You just phoned someone for help.'

'With all due respect, I think you must have imagined it.'

'The phone is literally still in your hand, sir.'

'No, it's not.'

The interviewers would inexorably be getting far more agitated by this point.

'So, are you telling me, you haven't been phoning someone, every time we ask you a question?'

McGuire would turn around once more.

'Jeff, I think they're onto us. They just asked me if I've been phoning you. What do I say?' He would turn to the interviewers again. 'I haven't even got a phone.'

And so it would continue, until the interviewer would lose all patience and profoundly declare the interview over.

Technique Two
Be Happy

Upon his research into effective interview techniques, McGuire once read that interviewers love enthusiasm from their prospective employees. As such, this was something he was keen to test out to see if it was true.

The enthusiasm in McGuire's case, however, was to be layered on so thick it would be strong enough to withstand a nuclear blast.

No matter **what** was said by the interviewer, after **every** question, statement, or gesture throughout the entire interview process, McGuire's reaction would always be the same. A deep and booming belly laugh, followed by a vigorous handshake and a high-five before he would start speaking in an excitable and over-enthusiastic manner which suggested he was currently living out the happiest moment of his life.

Even on the unfortunate occasions when the interviewers solemnly stated that the position had become unexpectedly made available due to a colleague's sudden death, the same overzealous belly laugh and high five would still be his response.

Within a few minutes of the interview, it would be guaranteed that the interviewers would have gone from thinking McGuire was a jolly and fervent fellow, to believing he was a fully-fledged lunatic.

Technique Three
Don't Lose the Plot

Another technique McGuire liked to call upon to mess with the minds of the interviewers was to incorporate plot lines from popular movies into his answers, when asked to give examples of things he had previously accomplished in various job roles.

'So, Mr McGuire,' an unsuspecting interviewer would begin. 'The job role you have applied for is a Project Manager. As such, you will be required to show strong leadership and role model behaviour on a daily basis. Can you provide me with any examples where you have previously shown strong leadership?'

'Sure thing, I guess a recent example I can think of where I've displayed strong leadership was when I inspired thousands of oppressed Scotsmen to take part in a rebellion against a tyrannical English king's rule and led them into a battle for their independence. They may take our lives, I told them. But they will not take our freedom.'

'That's a scene from Braveheart, Mr McGuire.'

'Brave what? Heart? Can't say I've ever heard of it.'

'If I can just take this opportunity to make the point that this is a serious interview, Mr McGuire. Shall we start again, maybe with a different question? As a Project Manager, you will be required to do a lot of planning, but inevitably things can sometimes go wrong and require great adaptability and thinking on your feet in correcting matters. Can you give me an example of when something you've planned has gone awry and you've had to act quickly in order to get things back on track?'

'That's a very good question, and one I'm only too pleased to answer. I guess one occasion that immediately springs to mind is when I was visiting my estranged wife, Holly, in New York at a Christmas party on the top floor of the building she was working in. Nakatomi Plaza. As bad luck would have it, the party was gate-crashed by a group of heavily armed international terrorists led by some German geezer called Hans Gruber. He was a bit of a buzzkill and was bringing everyone's mood down by shooting employees. I mean what a dick, right? I had no choice but to start picking off the group of terrorists one by one. What made it even more challenging was that all the while, I wasn't wearing any shoes. How embarrassing, right? Better than getting caught with your pants down though.'

'That's the plot to Die Hard,' the interviewer would sigh.

'What hard?' McGuire would respond innocently. 'I'm not sure I follow you.'

'Please leave.'

Technique Four

Dress for the Occasion

Most interviewers are impressed by someone who dresses fancy to an interview, so why can't they be impressed by someone who turns up in fancy dress? Talk about double standards.

A suit and tie are so cliché. If you really want to stand out from the crowd and make an impression, what better way than to turn up for said interview dressed as a Smurf or a Teletubby?

For bonus points, McGuire even liked to incorporate his costume into the interview by making this evident display of madness seem somehow plausible.

'Er, Mr McGuire, why have you come to an interview dressed up as Fred Flintstone?'

'Because I see myself as being the Bedrock of your company, sir, and I promise I will Yabba Dabba Do a great job for you.'

'Mr McGuire, why are you dressed up as an S&M gimp?

'Well, this job is for a Health and Safety awareness officer, is it not? And I'm all about spreading the importance of the safety word.'

'Um, Mr McGuire, I can't help but notice you've come to the interview in blackface and dressed up as Mr T. This is scandalous and outrageous. Not in any situation is this acceptable on any level. What the hell is going on?'

'It's because I see myself as being a key member of your A-Team, sir.'

Suffice to say, he never got offered any of the jobs.

Part Two

Opportunity Shocks

Scene One
Performance Art

A week had passed since McGuire's firing from Pet Names.

The time was approximately half past eleven in the morning, and he was busy in the spare room of his rented, two-bed, semi-detached house.

There were many in Chelmsley Green who were under the incorrect assumption that McGuire had been able to afford to rent this home by himself from benefits alone. Yet, the truth was his rent and other essentials had been mostly funded from the proceeds of numerous gambling sites.

Despite his antics, McGuire was an educated man, and had graduated from Oxford University with a degree in Mathematics.

One of the fields he had excelled in during these studies had been Statistics, and as such it assisted him greatly when placing the various bets to allow him a higher chance of winning and receiving an income enough to cover rent and continue playing his game. He never got greedy with these bets, however, and was always restrained enough to ensure he had enough in reserves should any poor run of form present itself.

McGuire was trawling through the various job search websites and recruitment agencies looking for his next potential unwitting victims.

The irony had not been lost upon him that his spare room resembled as much of an office as some of those he'd been fired from.

Aside from the computer monitor, keyboard, and high-quality printer placed on top his work desk, there was an adjacent filing cabinet to keep his numerous records and paperwork in - along with a stationary cupboard. There were even performance charts and targets scattered about the wall. He called them the Hall of Shame.

Amongst some of the categories upon his performance charts were the following statistics.

Angriest Customers

The winner for this category had been awarded to, The Patrons of the White Stag – a pub located in the town of Hamsgrove, approximately twelve miles south of Chelmsley Green.

The White Stag was tucked away, out of sight, in one of the side streets. The pub had gained itself, somewhat justifiably, a reputation as being an "old man's pub."

It was a Bermuda Triangle of drinking establishments. Its customers would enter at eleven in the morning when the bar would open and would not be seen again until eleven o'clock at night when the bar closed.

Its decades-old, nicotine-stained wallpaper, and cigarette-burned carpet, acted as a comfort blanket for the clientele. The bedraggled beer mats advertised breweries which had ceased to exist for close to a decade, and their only functional purpose these days was being wedged under the table legs to stop their wobbling as opposed to protecting the sticky and stained lager-lacquered tabletops.

McGuire's only day working at the White Stag had been in the role of a barman, and after an hour of tricking the landlord into thinking that he was capable of being left unsupervised for the remainder of his shift, he began to unleash the chaos.

'Do you have any ID?' he had asked an elderly gentleman who approached the bar asking for a round of bitter for each of his four friends sitting at one of the tables mid-game of Thirteen Card Brag.

At first, the pensioner laughed off this statement as merely benign banter from the new barman. Yet, as McGuire remained stone-faced in defiance, it was becoming clear to the old man that he was serious.

'I'm seventy-nine years old. I'm old enough to be your grandfather,' the elderly gentleman responded flabbergasted.

'With all due respect, sir, I only have your word for it that you're over eighteen. May I see your ID please?'

'But I don't carry any on me!'

'How convenient,' McGuire replied suspiciously. 'You can have a soft drink if you like, but that's the best I can do for you.'

'This is absurd,' the old man stropped as he trudged over to his table to inform his friends about the audacity of what had just happened.

After a brief cabinet meeting, one of the card-playing cronies at the table took it upon himself to approach the bar to ask for the sought-after round of beers.

Though the person asking for the ales was pushing eighty-two, the response was exactly the same.

'Have you got any ID sir?'

This pensioner was not so perplexed, having already been briefed about this stranger's behaviour. He had been fully prepared for it.

'As a matter of fact, I do, young man,' he declared victoriously as he smugly pulled out the driver's license from his wallet with as much victory as Arthur pulling Excalibur from the stone.

McGuire took the card and meticulously scrutinised the document for a painfully prolonged amount of time - approximately five minutes, in fact.

'I'm sorry sir, this is a fake ID,' he eventually declared. 'I'm going to have to confiscate it.'

As prepared as the pensioner thought he had been, it was evidently not enough as he became riled by McGuire.

'I assure you, young man, that document is very real, and I insist you give it back.'

'So you can try and hustle booze illegally from some other establishment?' McGuire countered. 'Not on my watch, kid.'

To confound matters further, a couple of men entered the pub and made their beeline straight to the bar, they couldn't have been much more than in their early twenties.

'What will it be gents?' McGuire asked enthusiastically.

'Two pints of Carling please,' the response came.

'Sure thing.'

The pensioner watched aghast as McGuire began to pour their beer without any challenge at all.

'What in the good lord's name is going on?' the old man astounded. 'Those two are over three times younger than I am and you didn't even ask them for ID.'

'That's because they don't look under eighteen,' the stern response came.

The pensioner went back to his table to join his aged allies in confoundment at their table.

It soon became a battle of the wits between the five pensioners and the bemusing barman. It was a Mexican Standoff with neither party willing to back down. At one point, McGuire had even threatened to ban the two twenty-somethings for ordering beers on the group of pensioner's behalf.

Half an hour had passed before the landlord, Roger Burton, came down to check on how McGuire was doing on his first shift. He didn't expect to be besieged by the five irate pensioners and their justified complaints about not being served.

'Barry, these men are clearly over eighteen, serve them now. Once again gents, I can only apologise for this misunderstanding. The next couple of rounds are on the house. Barry, please apologise to these men.'

'I'm sorry sirs,' McGuire professed begrudgingly. 'It's just I take underage drinking very seriously. My father was an underage drinker you see. He started drinking in pubs at five years old and it had a very negative impact on his life as you can imagine, I just don't want the same thing happening to anyone else if I can help it. What was it you wanted again?'

'Five pints of best,' one of the vindicated pensioners demanded. He was still unimpressed, and still very agitated - though the offer of free drinks softened the blow more than any apology or explanation.

'Of course, sir,' McGuire spoke affably as he poured five pints of lemonade instead for them.

'I think it's best you leave,' Roger ordered McGuire.

Most Confused Customers

This record went to those who had rung through on the customer service number of the motor insurance company, Nelson Prudential, and had been met with the misfortune of getting through to McGuire.

Usually, McGuire liked to find ways to get fired within the first day. But, on occasion, the opportunity for a dismissal so glorious meant having to play the long game. Well, a few days more in any case.

With call centre jobs, and especially those based in the finance sector, it is very rare for them to let you loose on the phones immediately. Intensive training, shadowing, and role-play are often required before being thrown into the lion's den.

The training itself had gone without incident for McGuire - if anything, he was a delight to instruct. Polite, charming, receptive, and quick at picking things up. Yet, like a tiger hiding from sight, in wait for his prey, he was simply biding his time. His time to pounce came four days later, when he was allowed to go onto live calls unsupervised for the first time.

'Good morning, you're through to Nelson Prudential, you're speaking to Barry McGuire, how can I help you today?' the perfectly courteous and professional greeting would come.

'Ah yes, good morning, I'm just calling through today to see if there are any discounts available if I renew my products with you.'

'Most certainly, I am more than happy to look into that matter for you, but before I do, can I interest you in making a little bit of extra money on the side? Cash in hand, tax-free, and all very hush hush of course.'

'Er, excuse me,' the confused reply would come.

'Well, working for Nelson Prudential is only my day job. I also do a bit of work on the side for some people who, for legal reasons, would prefer to stay anonymous. I mean some people, mainly the authorities, still tend to frown upon illegal organ harvesting. Anyways, long story short, their company, Liver Let Die, are on the lookout for young and healthy customers to assist them with their business.'

'Is there anyone else I can talk to, please? I'm only after a quote for renewing,' the perplexed voice would state.

'Of course, you "can" speak to someone else if you "really" want to, but answer me this with all honesty, would someone else on the line offer you this unique opportunity to make a few extra quid? If you make a verbal agreement with me today for my associates to take one of your kidneys at a time of our choosing, I promise you we'll make it worth your while. Besides, you don't need both your kidneys, so stop being so selfish.'

'Is this serious?' the befuddled caller would nervously ask.

'I kidney you not,' McGuire would then quip. 'Just some illegal organ harvesting humour there. If you can't laugh at having one of your organs removed against your knowledge, what can you laugh at? I can even offer you our hotel special and a cash payment of five hundred quid. Sure, you may wake up confused and in pain in a hotel bathtub full of ice with your body crudely operated on under makeshift anaesthetics, but at least you get a free hotel for the night, and we'll even throw in a complimentary continental breakfast.'

'You're insane, I only want a quote for Home and Contents.'

'Can I put you down as a maybe then?'

Needless to say, once the manager got wind of these calls, McGuire was promptly asked to leave.

Your friendly organ harvester is Barry McGuire

Liver Let Die

Fast Cash.
Discreet Organ Harvesting.
Breakfast included.

We pay great rates, we kidney you not.

Contact via
liverletdie@darkweb.com

Fastest Firing

This record was for an irresponsibly impressive seven minutes and took place in March of this year. The company in question was for a bespoke furniture manufacturing company, Stable Tops, and the position in question was as a Warehouse Worker.

The collective dumbfounded looks McGuire received from his co-workers as he walked through the warehouse doors for the first (and only) time was just a tease of the madness to come.

Although there had been no strict dress code indicated on the employee handbook he had been emailed prior to his starting, the outfit he was wearing was certainly not appropriate for work - or for most other places in this world for that matter.

'Whassup my mo-fo's,' McGuire spoke in an over-the-top stereotypical Harlem jive accent as he started high-fiving some of the aghast workers with his free hand. In his other hand, he clasped a snazzy cane. The outfit he was wearing was a purple, velvet, 70s Pimp costume.

'Where's all my fine-ass hos at?' he demanded loudly, yet jovially.

This derogatory question was not favourably received by the female members of staff on the warehouse floor - and they were not shy about sharing the justifiable offence they had taken. Although this comment was teetering close to violating Rule Number Six – Never Make things Personal, McGuire felt he could justify this comment as being exempt, due to it falling more in line with inappropriateness than direct harassment. Besides, it was more of a blanket enquiry than any targeted attack on any one person.

A group of the offended women stepped forward to confront McGuire. As intimidating and as justifiably fired up as they visibly were, he would not allow himself to break character. He had to be fearless in his game, and sometimes that even meant upping the performance.

'Hey women,' he addressed them in his jive accent. 'Not so much of the lip and calm it on the jip. Save your energy for your tricks when you give the customers those licks. Your jiving is hurting my brain, don't make me whack you with my cane.'

Their riled response and ensuing commotion was enough to bring the shift manager down from the comforts of his office and to ground zero of the maelstrom.

'What on earth is all this ruckus about?' the manager, a middle-aged man by the name of Gary Kimble yelled.

The group of offended women all started relaying their besmirchments towards Kimble, yet their agitated talking over one another as they addressed him made it impossible to decipher their words. What wasn't so hard for him to decode was that several of them were pointing to a man dressed up as a stereotypical pimp.

'Who the hell are you?' he asked.

'I'm Barry McGuire, the new pimp you hired. But you can call me, Sugarloaf MC,'

'I will do no such thing,' the unimpressed response came. 'McGuire? You're my new Warehouse Worker, aren't you?'

It was at this point McGuire allowed his proud expression to drop to one of confusion.

'Wait, Warehouse Worker, no no my Caucasian brother from a skanky mother, I'm your new Whorehouse Worker.'

'What!'

'It says so right here on the email you sent. I printed it off to bring with me.' McGuire reached into the pockets of his purple, velvet jacket and began to pull out the contents from within - most of which were unopened condom wrappers. Kimble looked on with simmering rage as McGuire began to hand over the prophylactics so he could carry on rummaging in his pockets. 'It said on the job description I had to be safety minded,' he spoke proudly as he acknowledged the condoms. 'Ah, here we are my main man.'

McGuire handed over a page of white A4 paper with an email printed out on it. Despite McGuire's smug look of, "I told you so," Kimble's was that of further disdain.

'You've scribbled out the word Warehouse and written Whorehouse in blue pen.'

'No I haven't,' McGuire argued.

'Then what do you call this?' Kimble waved the offending piece of paper in front of McGuire, pointing at the blatantly doctored word.

'Ah, ok, well, maybe I did change it to make the job sound more interesting. But even though it's out of whack, go throw your homie some brotherly slack.'

Fire McGuire – Steve McElhenny

'I want you out of here right now, and I never want to see you darken these doors again.'

Scene Two
Dog Days

McGuire was sitting at the desk of his spare room, filling out an application form for a store assistant at a popular supermarket chain, when suddenly, he was interrupted by the sound of a large and agitated dog barking and growling from downstairs.

There was in fact, no dog at all. The sounds were just a recording coming from a motion-sensor-activated re-recordable sound box he had purchased from eBay and installed in his hallway, close to the front door. Ever the practical joker, the reason for this contraption was purely for his unruly amusement, by messing with the mind of the local postman.

For McGuire, the practical joke had been long-running, and one he had committed himself to go all in on.

The motion sensor would be activated by the letterbox opening and the mail being pushed through. In the early days of his rambunctious ruse, the re-recordable sound effect would just be that of a yappy whiny dog. It was more of an irritant for the postman than any danger. Gradually, however, McGuire would evolve the recording to one more menacing and ferocious, until the soundtrack resembled something reminiscent of a wild beast. He would watch from his lounge window as the Postman nervously fumbled the mail through the letterbox, unknowingly setting off the sound effects before quickly retreating as fast as he could from the door in a panic, out of fear of losing not just a finger or two but his whole hand. For a while, McGuire even posted mail to himself just to cause the postman further duress.

After the sound of the ferocious and feral animal had stopped, McGuire made his way downstairs to retrieve whatever mail had been posted and could see that the offending item was that of an A4 manilla envelope. The return address on the back was that of a PO Box address located in London.

He partially withdrew the letter from its sheaf and could see in the top corner the logo of the toy company, Play Dates.

His first instinct upon seeing their logo was that it was a rejection letter to the application and CV he had sent them a week prior. His only surprise was that they had taken the time and effort to reply to him at all.

The vacancy he had applied for had been vague and confusing in its description, yet this was nothing unusual these days. It was becoming increasingly common with the jobs he was seeing advertised that their titles were being shit out by a random word generator. Director of First Impressions were what they were calling Receptionists now. Garbage men were Refuse Technicians and Administration Assistants are Secondary Task Specialists. It was getting to the point where you'd have more chance of breaking the Enigma Code than you would understanding what job you were actually applying for.

The Play Dates vacancy he had applied for was an Associate Product Architect for the Ideas and Development team. As best as he could decipher from the ostentatious title, and the much more linear job description, was that it was a very complicated way of saying, Product Designer.

Upon seeing this vacancy on one of the more upmarket job search websites a week earlier, he had placed it in the classification of jobs he would be unlikely to gain even an interview for. As such, he considered it as one of the subcategories of his larger game. In video game terms, it was the equivalent of a side quest if you will. And this particular mission was to mess with the minds of whoever was reading this CV as much as possible.

The content of the CV itself was undeniably impressive. Overly so, in fact. Highlights of which included some of the following achievements.

*Graduated with a first in Economics from Cambridge University.

*Project leader in a software development team for the London branch of Microsoft.

*Founder of several community outreach programs helping underprivileged youths become computer and financially literate.

*Helped design the world's first choke-free marble for toddlers.

In theory, this was certainly enough to get any perspective employer's interest piqued at the very least, and almost certainly enough to warrant an interview. In practice, however, McGuire had far greater methods to his madness.

Instead of typing up the resume and application on a Word doc and uploading it to the application page as was expected – and requested – McGuire wrote it out in red crayon. He had even made sure to place some of the letters the wrong way around, just as a five-year-old would. He then posted it via recorded delivery to the HR department.

McGuire wondered before reading the rejection letter whether it would gain a place hanging up on a designated section in his Hall of Shame for his best rejection letters. He had even taken the effort to frame them as if they were family portraits.

Yet, upon digesting the content of the letter, he felt as though the joke was on him. It was he who was left feeling dumbfounded and bewildered.

The letter was confirming his success in being shortlisted and making it to the interview stage. What's more, it was hand-signed by Sebastian Undergrove, the founder and managing director of Play Dates.

The interview, the letter stated, was to be at the company's headquarters in central London in seven days at

14:00.

On a good day, London was a two-and-a-half-hour commute from Chelmsley Green, and it involved a bus trip to the nearest town with a train station, and then another two changes on the connecting trains. The technical term for this kind of journey was, Massive Ball Ache.

Usually, such a long commute would be outside the playing field of McGuire's designated game zone. But just as he had to accept every job offer under the rules of his game, he also had to accept every interview. Besides, he reasoned to himself. It wasn't as if he had anything else better to do on that date.

> CV for BARRY McGUIRE
> aged 24 and a half :)
>
> QUALIFICASHUNS
> A+ FROM CAMBRIDGE UNIVERSITY
> PROJECT LEEDER for LONDON BRANCH of MICROSOFT
> FOUNDER of several Community outreach programs helping under priviliged youths become computer litterate.
>
> Helped design the Worlds first choke free Marble for toddlers
>
> I am hard working and great at stuff and would be a Assett to any Company
> love Barry
> xxx

Part Three

London Calling

Scene One
Let's Go on a Play Date

The time was a little past 13:15 when McGuire approached the headquarters of Play Dates LTD. It was a dowdy-looking, nine-story office building, whose unremarkable appearance was seeped in the epitome of drabness. To look at it from the outside, no one would believe that this was the place where so much creation and joy had found its origins.

Despite the exterior of the building's dowdy presentation, at least McGuire looked more eye-catching and livelier in his white suit and faded-black, MC Hammer: You Can't Touch This t-shirt, with an arrow below the text pointing towards his crotch.

Just like anyone readying themselves for an interview, McGuire had spent some time researching the company in preparation. The letter he'd received had initially thrown him off guard, and he didn't want to be unprepared for any surprises again. Not that he didn't know anything about the Play Dates' name already. Throughout his childhood, it had been a marquee brand in the toy industry. McGuire himself could even remember finding many hours of happiness as a child playing with some of their products. Yet now, like a once-great prize-fighter who had endured for so long, it had become a journeyman name, punch drunk and struggling to stay a relevant draw amongst its younger, stronger, and hungrier rivals.

His research had shown that the company had been founded by a gentleman named Sebastion Undergrove almost fifty years ago - and his creation of numerous early-education development toys had found great success in the market.

To say Undergrove was an overnight success in the industry wouldn't quite be correct. He had already been working hard for several years on designing and pitching products to the various market leaders - though he was met with nothing but rejections to show for his efforts.

In the end, according to his Wikipedia page, Undergrove decided that if he wanted his ideas to get to market, he would have to back himself and form his own toy company.

Putting up his family home as collateral, Undergrove took out a business loan. The gamble, subsidised by his incessant hard work, paid off. More and more of the smaller outlets began to stock his products until the larger franchises, supermarkets, and catalogue shops began to take notice and stock them too.

Play Dates soon became a known and trusted brand of quality and innovation, with several of their products even making it to the shortlist of many retailer's, Toy of the Year, category.

Those were better days for the company it would seem, and from what McGuire could determine, their presence in the industry was a far cry from what it had once been.

McGuire still hadn't decided on what interview technique he would use as he strode closer to the tinted glass automatic doors leading into the building. He had taken the stance that he would wait and get a sense of the situation first before playing one of his trump cards to cause havoc in the interview – of which he had amassed a whole deck's worth to call upon.

He stepped into the foyer and allowed himself a few moments to survey his surroundings. The atmosphere within the building was far warmer than the one it conveyed on its dreary exterior.

In his experiences since playing this game, he had learnt that you could gain a solid sense of what kind of company it would be like to work for by scanning the faces of the various employees as they shuffled back from their dinner breaks and returning to work.

The contented and smiling faces upon many of them indicated to McGuire that this was a good company to work for, and the large percentage of those he observed clearly enjoyed their jobs.

Directly facing him, once he had taken his first strides inside, was a reception desk with an attractive female receptionist sitting behind it, or as they were apparently known as now, a Director of First Impressions. She was aged in her early thirties, had shoulder-length blond hair, and had made the wise decision to wear very little makeup to accentuate her beauty - unlike some he'd seen who'd worn too much in the way of lipstick and eye shadow that they resembled more of a circus clown than a receptionist. If her title was indeed to direct a good first impression, then even the fiercest of critics would have to concede she was an auteur.

The smile this lady offered upon her face seemed a sincere and natural fit.

'Good afternoon,' she confidently spoke pre-empting McGuire's approach to her station. 'Can I be of some help to you today?'

'Good afternoon,' he replied as he made his way over to her. 'I'm hoping you **can** be of some help actually. I have a job interview this afternoon and I'm not entirely sure where I need to go, or who I need to report to.'

'Certainly, sir,' her amiable reply came. 'I'll just need to phone through upstairs to let them know you've arrived, and someone will come down and collect you. May I take your name please?'

'Sure, it's Barry McGuire.'

The receptionist politely nodded her head to show that she had digested this information.

McGuire watched as she typed in his name on the keyboard with an impressive speed and pressed the Return key. As she read the information that was brought up on her computer monitor, her eyes widened with keen interest that suggested the information relayed was not what she had expected. She cleared her throat then picked up the receiver on her desk phone and pressed a solitary button on the handset. McGuire observed that the button she'd pressed had a gold star stuck to it and was the only button upon the handset that had any kind of sticker at all. McGuire briefly wondered what made this dialled hotline so special. Was it connected to some kind of Batphone? He observed the young woman compose herself slightly as she waited for a response.

'It's Kimmy from the front desk. Mr McGuire has arrived for his interview. I have a note on his appointment that you wanted to be notified.'

Kimmy stayed on the line for a while longer as she listened to a side of the conversation that McGuire wasn't privy to. He couldn't help but notice that even though her unmovable smile didn't falter, the look of astonishment conveyed by her raised eyebrows suggested something of interest may have just been relayed to her. She placed down the phone and quickly began using the computer monitor as a makeshift mirror to needlessly check and tidy her immaculate appearance. She then turned her attention to Barry.

'Mr Undergrove will be here to collect you shortly.'

The surprised tone in her voice indicated that this wasn't a regular occurrence, especially to escort interviewees.

'As in Sebastion Undergrove?' he sought to clarify.

Kimmy nodded.

'He's a wonderful man,' she continued.

Despite her praise and evident admiration of her employer, there was a tone of sadness present in her voice which McGuire couldn't help but pick up on. The reason why became apparent approximately five minutes later.

McGuire saw a frail and gaunt gentleman walking slowly towards them. This person was relying far too heavily on a custom-made wooden cane with a crest of a silver owl below the handle.

Undergrove stopped a couple of times during the short pilgrimage from the first of the two elevators in the foyer to the reception desk. The reason for his halt was so he could regain his breath following several coughing fits filled with gusto - along with traces of blood-speckled phlegm projected into the handkerchief he had pulled out of his suit jacket.

Although he was aged in his early seventies, he looked to be around twenty years older, and McGuire noted only a passing resemblance to the photograph of the proud, distinguished-looking man on his Wikipedia page.

'Lung cancer,' Kimmy whispered subtly to McGuire from the desk. Partly to satisfy any curiosity McGuire may have held, and partly to stop him potentially putting his foot in his mouth by asking Mr Undergrove directly.

Despite his struggles, Undergrove tried his hardest to maintain his look of happiness as he approached.

'Mr McGuire, I presume,' he spoke with impish glee as he extended his hand for him to shake. 'Come, let's get you to your interview.'

'Maybe you should take a few minutes to sit down first, Mr Undergrove,' Kimmy interjected protectively.

'Firstly, as I keep telling you Kimmy, Mr Undergrove was my father, you can call me Sebastian. Secondly, as much as I appreciate your concern, I'll have more than enough opportunity to rest my bones when I'm dead and buried. I want to get as much done now while I still can, and I won't achieve that by taking a seat for a few minutes. Life waits for no man, and no man should wait to live their life.'

Undergrove turned his attentions back towards McGuire.

'Come, Barry,' won't you come and indulge an old dying man for a short while?'

Undergrove gestured for McGuire to follow him.

'If I'm walking too fast for you to keep up let me know and I'll slow down,' Undergrove quipped mischievously before letting out a laugh, followed by another involuntary cough. He gestured with his cane towards the left-hand-side elevator. 'We're going to the seventh-floor meeting room for your interview. The two gentlemen interviewing you are a good sort and you'll be in capable hands. I'll be there too observing, but purely as a silent witness. Well, as silent as one can be with this infernal cough of mine, but I hope it doesn't distract you too much. Even though I like to personally read every application and CV that passes through these doors, and I have the final say in whittling down the candidates, I don't like to get involved in the interview process and final decision. I like to put my trust in my staff's judgement, and I will on this one too. But, when I read your application and CV, it's fair to say it gained my interest, which is why I wanted to come down and meet you in person. When you get to the final months of your life, anything that makes you smile is a priceless gift, so whatever happens in that interview I just want to say a personal thank you.'

His speech became halted by another series of coughs before he composed himself.

'Now, let's not bullshit each other here. I may be knocking very loudly on death's door but I'm not an idiot. Anyone with an ounce of sanity could tell that you haven't achieved any of those things you stated on your application, and that is why I shortlisted you. The world is evolving at a worryingly rapid rate Barry, and you will never keep up with it by maintaining the status quo. I've had hundreds of applications from fine, ambitious, and accomplished individuals, who unlike you, do have the experience and knowledge in product design and development. And therein lies my quandary. When I saw your CV written in red crayon like a child, I had an epiphany. No child has a degree in engineering or experience in market research. But…every child has an imagination and that is what we need here. Give me one person with imagination over a thousand with ambition any day. Now, chances are, you only sent that application off for a laugh, maybe as a dare or a prank with some of your buddies. But the fact you're here now says you're serious enough about it to give it a shot.'

McGuire simply smiled at Undergrove.

His first impressions were that he liked this man very

much, but he couldn't let geniality or sympathy distract him. He was still playing his game, and this was just another job for him to get fired from. But first, he had to get hired.

Undergrove ushered McGuire to the elevator door using his cane as if it were a shepherd's crook, and McGuire was his sheep. He used the base of the cane to press the up button on the lift, and both men entered.

McGuire couldn't help but hear a tune playing over the speakers within the lift. It was a child-like jingle and one he could only assume was the theme tune for the company. A chorus of toddlers sang the words to a melody that sounded like that of an old Jack in the box.

'We play while we learn and learn while we play.'

'We're all going on a Play Date today.'

The tune and the lyrics repeated themselves on a loop, throughout the elevator's ascent to the seventh floor.

'What do you think of the jingle, Barry? And be honest with me, I demand nothing less from my staff.'

'It's a shame we're not getting off on the third floor instead,' McGuire quipped dryly.

Undergrove didn't appear to take any offence, and instead let out a hearty laugh, which resulted in another chesty cough.

'This building has nine floors in total, but we only have staff on the top three these days. The other floors we lease out to other companies. Needs must I'm afraid, and the extra income helps us to just about keep our heads above water. I hope I'm not scaring you off with the bleak outlook for this company's future.'

McGuire shook his head. One way or another he would be gone from this building long before the company was.

The elevator came to a halt and McGuire exited it in haste to escape that infernal jingle. Not that he felt his evacuation would make any difference, it was likely to be stuck in his head for a long time to come.

Undergrove escorted him to the door of a waiting room, shook his hand and wished him the best of British.

Scene Two
The Wait of Expectations

McGuire made his way into a generic-looking waiting room where he counted two men and a lady. They were each engrossed by their phone screens, deep in concentration - most likely getting in those last-minute notes and research. When this trio did look up at him, they scoffed to themselves as they laid eyes upon his attire. Not seeing him as any kind of substantial rival for the vacant position, they reverted their eyes to their phones and gave his presence amongst them no further consideration.

It would have been easy for McGuire to mess with this trios' minds and throw them off their focus, yet another of the subrules to the game he had imposed upon himself for interviews was that he could never sabotage anyone else's chances or performance in order to gain an advantage. As such, all he could do for now was wait.

He was summoned approximately half an hour after his arrival. Two of the candidates that had been in the waiting room when he'd arrived had been and gone, making it approximately fifteen minutes for an interview.

When interviews were that short, in McGuire's extensive experiences, it usually meant only one of two things. Either the process was just a formality and they'd already had someone shoehorned in mind and were simply going through the facade to appease internal legislations. Or there were so many candidates that it had become an assembly line of interviews, trying to get through all the candidates in as little time as possible. In either scenario, it only reinforced the notion in his mind that he was simply there to make up the numbers. Especially given Undergrove's proclamation that he would have no input in the final decision.

The middle-aged, slender-framed gentleman who had

been summoning the candidates from the waiting room and escorting them to the interview arrived back into view of the open doorway. He called out McGuire's name. He was smartly dressed in a navy suit with a cream shirt and peacock-patterned tie.

The tone in which this gentleman summoned McGuire was performed in a courteous enough manner despite it being clear from his incongruous body language and languid handshake that he had already made up his mind about this applicant from the travesty of the CV he had read from him. He evidently lacked the same epiphany over its presentation as Mr Undergrove.

'My name is Giles Hensley, it's a pleasure to meet you.' He introduced himself somewhat robotically in his well-practiced spiel as he led McGuire to the interview room. 'The interview will be conducted by myself and my colleague, Harris Singer. Our founder and managing director, Sebastian Undergrove will also be in attendance, but will be there purely as a fly on the wall. Just pretend he isn't there. Our interviews tend to be more casual and informal than most other companies. All we ask is that you be yourself and answer the questions with honesty and to the best of your abilities. That all being said, are you ready Barry?'

'Ready to blow your minds,' he returned with a smile.

Scene Three
Open to Interpretation

The interview room was set up with a black-cloth-covered table with a jug of iced water garnished with a couple of wedges of lemon and a tray of clean drinking glasses to offer to the interviewees, should they want some refreshments. The table had two chairs placed behind it, one of which was already occupied by a man whom McGuire correctly assumed to be Harris Singer. In the corner of the room sat Undergrove who did little to acknowledge McGuire upon his entering the room. He wasn't exaggerating when he said he would have no involvement in the interview process.

After a brief greeting from Singer, McGuire sat himself down. There was an uncomfortable silence as the interviewers quickly revisited the CV. It was clear from their expressions that they couldn't wait to get this interview over and move on to more deserving applicants.

McGuire already knew how they thought this interview was going to play out in their minds. Oh, how wrong they were going to be.

Having already been resigned to the fact that this was a job offer that would be eluding him, something Undergrove had said returned itself to his mind.

'When you get to the final months of your life, anything that brings an unexpected smile to your face is a genuine gift.'

Though he would never consider himself to be a good Samaritan, McGuire was always more than willing to do a good deed whilst playing his game if the situation permitted – and he could think of no better situation to give Undergrove a parting gift.

'So, Mr McGuire,' Singer spoke upon placing the CV back on the table. 'It's quite the résumé. I would like to point out that employment at Play Dates is one of the most fun and spiritually rewarding jobs one would ever be fortunate enough to have in this short life of ours. Nonetheless, the role you are applying for is one of great responsibility - both to the company and to the children whom we're targeting our products. Now, I appreciate a sense of humour as much as the next person, but this application screams to me of someone who doesn't take that responsibility seriously. What assurances can you give me that you're approaching this whole process with earnest?'

'Which one of you two is called Earnest again?' McGuire quipped.

There was a slight chuckle from the corner of the room, followed by an involuntary cough.

'Sorry,' Undergrove addressed his two employees. 'Just a bit of trapped wind. I'm not here, remember. Please, carry on.'

'You're not helping refute our point,' Hensley spoke sternly.

McGuire couldn't help but think that Hensley's earlier declaration that their interviews were a lot more casual than others was nothing but hogwash, or at least in McGuire's instance. These two fancied themselves as a couple of grizzled veteran police officers interrogating their suspect in a second-rate TV cop show. Only the reality was they were more Keystone Cops than Good Cop Bad Cop

'My apologies,' the interviewee's reply came. 'Rest assured I'm taking this whole interview with all the seriousness it deserves. Please allow me to answer your question about just how profoundly I'm taking it in the best way I know how. Sometimes words can't tell the whole story. But interpretive dance can.'

McGuire bounded from his chair and thrust his right arm aloft in the air before slowly bringing it down again, fist clenched. He then bent forward, almost horizontally, arms stretched outwards towards the duo of bemused men behind the desk. He then shuffled backwards in something close to resembling a moonwalk, before launching into an expressive dance routine.

The awkwardness of what was happening in front of Singer and Hensley's eyes was made even more so by the duration of the "dance" routine. It had already been going on for over ten minutes and was showing no sign of abating. By this point, McGuire had found even more ways to add to the madness by humming his own theme tune as he danced. That wasn't enough for him though, and before the end of the act, he had even progressed into singing a full-blown song to go with the dance. The term "Song" in this instance, was a very loose interpretation of the word. There was no coherent tune, no identifiable sentence structure, nor was there even any attempt at rhyming. It was just a series of random statements he was belting out in a borderline melodic fashion. He was putting the verse into perverse.

'I'm Barry McGuire and I'll be the best employee you've ever had.

I'm singing my song in front of my two new best friends Singer and Hensley, though I can't remember if one of them was called Earnest or not, I wasn't really paying that much attention to them.

I like making toys, they are lots of fun, so is crazy golf, I hope to play some one day with Singer and Hensley because we are best friends now.

I hope that one of them marries my sister and the other gets to be best man at their wedding.'

And so, the nonsensical musical ramblings would continue, along with the dance moves that made equally as little sense.

The only thing that was preventing Singer and Hensley putting a much-desired halt to this farce was the sound of chuckling, and on occasion, genuine belly laughter from Undergrove in the corner of the room. They hadn't seen their employer display so much joy for a long time, and for that reason alone they whispered to each other in consultation that they would simply let McGuire continue until he either got bored or tired himself out - much like the toddlers their company designed the toys for. It was eighteen long minutes until that moment finally came.

'So,' McGuire panted, genuinely out of breath from his efforts. 'I think we can all agree I nailed that interview. When do we start talking about my company car and a pay rise?'

Scene Four
Executive Division

The time was a little after half-past-four.

Singer and Hensley had been deep in debate over the interviews of the day when they became interrupted by a knock at the door of their shared office. Any questions they may have had about the identity of who had perpetrated the knock were soon answered by the unmistakable sound of uncontrollable coughing.

Hensley was quick to get up to his feet and open the door to their boss as Singer pulled out a chair. Whether or not he was staying long for his visit was a moot point, there was no doubt he would still require a seat.

'Bastian,' Hensley greeted. 'Is everything ok?'

'Aside from the obvious, everything is hunky-dory, Giles. I just thought I'd swing by and see how you were getting on after the interviews today. Looked like there were some mighty fine candidates.'

'It was certainly an interesting day that's for sure, but yeah we're really optimistic we've got some good eggs in there.'

Undergrove struggled over to the chair that had been pulled out for him and began to survey some of the notes on the table.

'Who are you thinking, gents?'

'Well,' Singer spoke. 'It looks like we've narrowed it down to Elizabeth Frost and Dennis Sutherland. They both have great experience, are very amiable people, and would fit straight in with our team at Ideas and Development.'

Hensley nodded his head in agreement.

'Honestly Bastian, it's that close, I think it could come down to a coin toss.'

'What about Barry McGuire? I see he hasn't made it to your shortlist?'

His two employees emitted a hefty laugh in symmetry, one which subsided into one of awkward confusion as they surveyed Undergrove's deadpan face.

'You're being serious!' Singer exclaimed rather than questioned.

'Well, why not?' the boss's reply came.

'Do you want my honest opinion?'

'Always. You know our mantra here - An honest opinion is the only opinion that matters.'

'With McGuire, there are only two logical explanations that would explain his conduct throughout his entire candidacy. Either there's some significant mental health issues going on there, or he's just making a mockery over our recruitment process.'

'I don't for one second think he's mentally unwell,' Undergrove contributed.

'In that case,' Hensley interjected. 'He's just a clown with far too much time on his hands.'

'Maybe,' Undergrove conceded. 'But let me put this to you. He's got something that no amount of education or experience can teach. You gentleman appear to be forgetting one of the first lessons I gave when I hired you all those years ago. Look at profits through the eyes of a businessman but look at life through the eyes of a child. That's what I was doing throughout today.

Ask yourselves this. If eight-year-old versions of yourself were interviewing today, would your shortlist be the same as it is now? Do you think an eight-year-old would care about experience in market research or product development? Or do you think they would care more about who made them laugh and smile? Yes, McGuire is a clown, there can be no disputing that. But, at the end of the day, if life truly is a circus, is it not the clowns who reign supreme?'

'You're really pulling for this guy, aren't you Bastian?' Singer said.

'I just think we need to try something different. Putting

our business heads back on for a minute, it's no secret that for the last few years, our products have been underperforming at a worrying rate, and we've been haemorrhaging money as a company as a consequence. Sure, those who've applied are impressive, but so were their predecessors. The very definition of madness is trying the same thing over and over again and expecting different results. We need to try something different and leftfield soon, or I fear this company as it stands won't survive for much longer, and you know my dying wish is to see Play Dates return to its former glory before I leave this mortal coil.'

'I'm calling it now. He wouldn't last a week here,' Singer countered.

'Very possibly. And if he doesn't, then it's only a week we've lost. I think that's a gamble well worth taking a punt on. If you bet on a five-hundred-to-one outsider and it comes up trumps, then aren't the rewards undeniable? But, as always gentlemen, I put all my trust and faith in you to make the correct decision. All I'm doing is adding my opinions into the mix.'

Undergrove bid farewell for the day and exited the office, leaving Singer and Hensley an unexpected decision to make. Whether to go with their instincts and every ounce of logic they held or go with the worst candidate they had ever witnessed on a hunch of their boss. A boss who was enduring the final months of his deteriorating health.

In the end, they begrudgingly submitted to their boss's wishes.

What was the worst that could happen?

Part Four

The First Day

Fire McGuire – Steve McElhenny

Scene One
The Jackson (P-Forty) Five

McGuire had left his home a smidgen before 06:00, in order to catch the first bus leaving from Chelmsley Green. It was the only way for him to make it to the nearest connecting train to arrive in London in time for the 09:00 start – and he didn't want to be late for getting fired on his first day of the job. Besides, the way he saw it, if he was going to London for the day, why not make the most of it and get some sightseeing and museums done too after his inevitable sacking?

Due to the early hour, there weren't many passengers on the bus. Yet, those who were, despite their tired morning eyes, couldn't help but sneak a glance at McGuire's eye-catching outfit. It was a look he anticipated he would be seeing more of once he made it to a more populated transport and hour of day.

He was dressed up with various incarnations of Michael Jackson attire, complete with a replica of his iconic red leather jacket from the Thriller video, and the trademark glove. After all, he was working in a toy company, was he not? And who loved little boys more than Jacko? Allegedly.

A week earlier, he would have been more than confident that his attire alone would have been enough to set him off on the wrong foot with his new employers. Yet, a week earlier he would never have envisaged that his antics during the interview would have seen him offered this job.

As much as he was loathe to admit it, doubts were lingering in his mind about whether he had underestimated this company and how easy it would be to get fired from them. The more confident and dominant side of him quelled these thoughts as best they could, however. This was just a toy company after all - and with his ingenuity and audacity, surely a sacking within the first day was a mere formality. Maybe, he'd even earn himself some new records to put on his Hall of Shame.

The time was 08:50, and McGuire entered the foyer of the Play Dates headquarters.

The familiar and welcoming face of Kimmy greeted him from behind the reception desk. Surely with her first impressions already performed, her job title had now been relegated to Director of Second Impressions.

'Good morning, Kimmy,' McGuire spoke.

Despite her smile not shifting from her permanently fixed position, he could see that the receptionist couldn't quite remember him. And why should she? She must have seen no end of strangers walking through these doors on a daily basis.

'It's Barry McGuire. Today's my first day,' he said, saving her the awkwardness of having to ask his name.

'Oh, yes,' she recalled. 'Welcome to our Play Dates family.'

'If we're part of the same family now, have you ever considered incest?' he thought of saying - and perhaps would have done had it not fallen under the sexual harassment umbrella of rule number six. Instead, he just returned the smile.

She rummaged through one of the desk drawers and pulled out a work pass and lanyard. She typed something onto the keyboard of her PC and her eyes examined something on the monitor.

'Mr Undergrove has requested that you go and see him in his office before he introduces you to your new team.'

'He's pretty hands-on in this company, isn't he?' Barry probed.

'Very much so. He's never had any wife or kids and this place has been his life. I guess when you're that involved and attached, it's hard to let go. Especially with, well, his health. He probably wants to make sure this place is in the best of order before he leaves us.'

McGuire noticed the impossible had happened when Kimmy spoke this last sentence. Her smile had faltered.

'He's on the ninth floor, his office is the last one along the corridor.'

McGuire entered the left-hand elevator and was instantly greeted by that infernal Play Date jingle as the doors closed. He pressed the button for floor nine. If it wasn't for rule number three – No destruction of property, he would have smashed the speaker playing that abomination of a song there and then.

He followed Kimmy's instructions and made his way to the office at the end of the corridor.

Upon knocking politely at the door, he felt certain he could say or do something in Undergrove's presence to warrant an immediate firing, yet he felt it best to leave him directly out of his game as best he could, the poor bastard was suffering enough as it was.

'Enter,' the weak-sounding voice came. Upon seeing McGuire, Undergrove stood up to greet him, and extended his frail hand. 'So good to see you, my boy,' he stated jovially.

'McGuire smiled and returned the embrace.

Undergrove's attention turned to his new employee's attire and produced a sincere smile.

'Looking very snazzy, I may say Barry. I've never been one for following the fashion trends of those much younger and cooler than myself, but I've got to say it looks very eye-catching and vibrant. I may have to adopt it as our dress code for all the staff. I bet the young boys and girls would love it.'

'You have no idea!' McGuire rued aloud. Yet his thoughts travelled along a different path. Either this guy was the sweetest man in the world or a demented evil genius who was trolling him for all his worth.

'So, before I take you to meet your new teammates, who I'm sure you're going to love,' Undergrove continued. 'We need to get some of the boring administrative stuff out of the way. I just have a few documents to hand over to you to read and sign, such as your employee contract. Just the usual stuff in there, job description, emergency contacts, holiday entitlement, sick policy, salary, behavioural expectations in the workplace etc. If you want to have a good read through it when you get a spare ten minutes and sign it off for our records in your own time. Technically, you're not an employee here until you do.'

'In that case, I may as well get it out of the way now.'

McGuire gave the documents a read. Although it didn't take the ten minutes Undergrove suggested, his reading of them were still very thorough. Whereas some employees just tend to skim these kind of docs with indifference or haphazardness, for McGuire, he found employee handbooks a valuable insight into the company's mindset and culture. It was almost like reading a detective story and the clues to cracking the case were hidden in plain sight. Once satisfied with the contents within, he put pen to paper and scrawled his name on the back page in the space provided.

'Alright then, I can now officially say to you, welcome to the Play Dates family. It's great to have you on board. I hope you won't mind me saying, but I've really stuck my neck out in recommending you for this job. I just hope my faith will be rewarded.'

McGuire said nothing in reply to this.

'Right, we'll have plenty of time throughout the day to have a natter and get to know one another a little better, I'm sure. But, for now, I know your team are chomping at the bit to meet you, so let's not keep them waiting any longer.'

Scene Two
Son-of-a-pitch

McGuire was led to a room on the eighth floor of the building. Had it not been for Undergrove's struggles, he would have gladly taken the stairs, but as it was, he had to endure that elevator once more. Though the time inside was thankfully short, it was still enough to hear that pretty-shitty-ditty a couple times more.

'We play while we learn and learn while we play.'

'We're all going on a Play Date today.'

'Have you thought of any alternative words to the jingle yet?' Undergrove asked mischievously as they left. 'And don't forget, Barry, an honest opinion is the only opinion we value here.'

'Oh, er, no I haven't actually. I've been trying to block that travesty of a tune out of my mind.'

Undergrove laughed.

'You will soon enough, almost everyone has their own version of it. Most of them unfit for the young ears it was intended for.'

'What's your version?' McGuire asked.

Undergrove smiled and cleared his throat. For once it wasn't as a result of his coughing. He began to sing the jingle.

'I hate this tune; it makes me want to burn my ears. I've had to listen to this shit for far too many years.'

Undergrove and McGuire approached a door to an office room which had the sign Ideas and Development Team – Where ideas are Played out.

Undergrove rapped at the door with his cane and opened it before any reply could come.

The chorus of greetings that met their boss as he entered were genuine in their joy at seeing him. McGuire gave a quick survey of his surroundings and saw that five desks were present within the spacious room. Four of the desks were occupied, he deduced the empty one, closest to the window, must have been for himself.

His four new colleagues stood up in symmetry and made their way over to make their formal introductions.

McGuire's first impressions were that they were an eclectic bunch. Not so much the odd couple, but the queer quartet.

The eldest of the team was a male aged in his early-to-mid fifties. He wore a garish green suit along with a red bowtie and matching trouser braces set. Even with his Michael Jackson outfit, McGuire suddenly felt that he wasn't the most foolishly dressed in the room. His gormless, acne-scarred face was dominated by an oversized, thick-rimmed set of circular framed glasses, also in red to match his bowtie and braces. McGuire guessed he wore these to draw attention away from the blemishes of his face.

As this man enthusiastically shook McGuire's hand, he introduced himself as Jerry Finch. He also stated he was the manager of the team.

The second person to introduce themselves was another male, and he was of a similar age to McGuire. He introduced himself as Jaycon Yates and was keen to make a point of his forename being spelled with a C instead of an S.

McGuire wanted to point out that this didn't make his name cooler, it just made his parents either illiterate or just plain didn't like him and wanted him to suffer a lifetime of ridicule. Yet he elected to hold his tongue on pointing this out to him. Rule Six: Never Get Personal.

Jaycon sported short, dark brown hair with a long quiffed fringe fixed firmly in place with so much wax, his hair could have its own exhibit in Madam Tussauds. His facial look was completed by a styled moustache that would not have looked amiss in a Wild West movie. His facial stylings were completed by an immaculately groomed shorter beard. McGuire observed that a vape pen was half visible, protruding from his skinny jeans pocket. He suspected it had been strategically placed in that position as a fashion accessory over any smoking addiction. The t-shirt he sported was a Misfits t-shirt, and McGuire doubted that Jaycon with a C had ever listened to a Misfits track in his life, let alone being able to name one. On top of the t-shirt, he wore an open grey suit jacket. He had the aura of hipster written all over him. Whoever he was trying to impress, McGuire certainly wasn't one of them.

'Interesting outfit,' Jaycon stated as he examined the newcomer's attire with intrigue.

'Yeah, I thought I'd get down with the kids,' McGuire's sarcastic retort came. Not that he felt sure the sardonic reply was fully picked up. He even began to suspect that Jaycon was examining him for fashion tips.

The third person to introduce themselves was aged in her late thirties, yet her clothing would suggest that she was much older. She was a conservatively dressed woman by the name of Tina Purfoyle. Her handshake was very timid, and her persona was equally demure. Tina's verbal greeting was soft and barely audible. McGuire sensed obtaining a HR complaint for inappropriate behaviour from her would be an easy task to achieve. She was a small, skittish bird in the presence of a hungry snake.

McGuire couldn't have been happier about the selection of colleagues he had been thrown in with. He was feeling even more confident about getting the latest round of his game wrapped up in double quick time.

Then, the fourth and final member of his new team introduced herself.

She was a beautiful, auburn-haired woman, aged in her early thirties. Despite her casual clothing she still looked incredibly elegant.

'I'm Victoria Barker,' she tersely stated.

Though she tried her hardest to be polite, McGuire could see the disapproval in her eyes. He was a good enough reader of body language to know that the contempt she was inadvertently projecting wasn't just of his outfit, but of him as a complete package. She obviously had good instincts.

'Well, you've been given the perfect day to start Barry,' Jerry gushed. 'Today's the day we get to pitch the ideas we've been working on for the past few months to an audience of potential investors and a specially selected focus group. It will be a great opportunity for you to see what we do here and what we're trying to achieve. Hopefully, all going well, you'll get to do a pitch of your own someday soon in the near future.'

Never one to let an opportunity go to waste, McGuire was quick to pounce.

'I can pitch one today if you like.'

He could see the look of confoundment engraved upon his new colleague's faces.

'I admire your enthusiasm,' Jerry returned diplomatically. 'But pitches like ours take months to prepare for. We have months of careful research to do. Product design and safety tests, financial and manufacturing logistics, and that's before the product even makes it to the prototype stage we have ready for today.'

'Nah, it'll be fine,' McGuire countered nonplussed by Jerry's words, purposely raising the ire of his colleagues. 'I can knock something up for a pitch by lunchtime, it'll be a piece of cake.'

The sound of a cough rang through the air.

For a short while, they had forgotten Undergrove was still in the room.

'Let him do his pitch, Jerry.' Undergrove spoke. 'We've paid for the focus group for the whole afternoon, we may as well utilize them for all that time. If Barry can't get something together by then, we're in no worse a position, are we?'

'Well, no, I guess not.' Jerry yielded.

'Besides, he's got me intrigued now, to see what he can

come up with in such a short amount of time. In any case, you **all** have a lot to do before lunch, and I'm sure you're going to ace it. I'm not the kind of person who enjoys putting extra pressure on you guys, especially in light of recent tragedies. So, you don't need me to tell you how much we need a win today. If not for myself or the company, let's do it for Niles. I'll see you all later at the focus group.'

Scene Three
Occupational Hazards

The time was coming up to 14:00 and McGuire had finally come back from his lunch, a lunch that started at 10:00.

He had managed to convince Jerry to let him have a few hours out of the office to allow him to source materials to help him with his pitch.

McGuire was uncertain as to whether Jerry would always be this much of a soft touch to get around, or if it was merely a one-off exception because there was so much work for the team to do to prepare for their respective pitches that afternoon, and he was just grateful to not have the extra distraction of having to answer the new-starter's questions all morning. McGuire suspected it was the former, but in either case, he wasn't planning on being around long enough to find out.

Usually, he wouldn't have liked to sacrifice four productive hours of potential firing time to be out of the workplace. Yet, in this instance, an idea had popped into his head. One that was so audacious it was worth waiting the extra hours for. If he managed to pull off this plan how he envisioned it, there would surely be a new achievement going up on his Hall of Shame for, Most Outlandish Firing.

McGuire took the strenuous flight of stairs up to the eighth floor and made his way to his office. Despite his plan to avoid the elevator whenever possible, it already seemed like an exercise in futility. Just thinking about that damned lift was enough for that wretched jingle to get stuck on a loop inside his mind.

Upon returning to his office, he was instantly met with a look of scorn from Victoria.

'Been working hard I see,' she scoffed. Purposely loud enough to catch Jerry's attention.

McGuire had by now ditched his Whacko Jacko attire.

It wasn't causing the reaction he was hoping for anyway. It was time for him to try a new tactic to rile his colleagues. He had returned to the office wearing a new garb.

A baseball cap from Madame Tussauds.

A T-shirt from the Natural History Museum.

A new lanyard for his security pass from the London Dungeon.

And a Tote bag from the Sealife London Aquarium.

Any hope he had that Jerry would catch wind of Victoria's haranguing was misplaced, however. Their manager was too deep in reading his notes to pay any attention. Oh, how he wished Victoria was his manager instead.

'When in Rome,' McGuire responded to her nonchalantly, purposely raising her ire. Even when her face was flush with anger, he couldn't deny her beauty.

'Well, you're not in Rome, are you?' she bit. 'You're meant to be working. You may not be taking this job seriously, but the rest of us are. We've worked too damned hard and lost too damned much for today to be in vain.'

She stormed back to her desk and picked up some pages upon her desk. They were almost as ruffled as she was.

'Hey, Bazza,' Jayce spoke quietly as he gestured for him to approach his desk. 'Don't take it personally,' he whispered. 'She's actually a really sweet person when you get to know her. She's just not been herself as of late. She still hasn't gotten over what happened to Niles. Well, none of us have really, but she's taken it the hardest for sure.'

Barry threw the hipster a sincere look that said, 'Am I supposed to know what you're talking about?'

Jayce was quick to pick up on McGuire's expression, he was clearly more astute than he had initially given him credit for.

'Oh yeah, sorry,' he whispered. 'First day and all. You're not to know. Niles Malone was your predecessor. Victoria and he were pretty tight. Some would say, a little bit too tight, if you know what I mean. Though they never officially declared it to the workplace, we all knew they were dating. He was a pretty cool dude. Proper switched on, and really going places in the world. Well, that was until...his passing. He had developed a product that went to market. It scored well with all the focus groups and the investors were really excited over it. It had a lot of money put into the marketing campaign, and the company was pinning a lot of hopes on it, but sadly it just didn't connect with the children or the consumers and it kinda flopped massively.

    Despite Sebastian's insistence that it wasn't his fault, Niles took its failure and the loss of all that time and money very personally. I guess the guilt and the stress of the whole situation got too much for him, and so did his drinking. We hoped that it was just a phase, and he would get back to himself soon enough, but if anything, he seemed to get worse. Not that we helped matters in hindsight. Jerry had no choice but to let him go, and poor Victoria told him that until he got his act together, she would be severing ties with him too. Anyways, long story short, he had gotten himself highly intoxicated one morning and the poor bastard flung himself in front of a moving train.'

    'Jesus, that's awful,' McGuire spoke - and meant it. Jayce's story resonated with him only too strongly. McGuire too had lost someone to taking their own life. His elder foster brother, Joseph, a little over three years earlier.

    'Yeah, so as I said,' Jayce continued, bringing McGuire's attention back to the room. 'Don't take it personally. Whoever came into this job, Victoria would have a hard time accepting.' Jayce slapped him on the shoulder reassuringly. 'So, are you really going to pitch a product this afternoon? Man, that's pretty ballsy on your first day and all. If this is a power play, then that's a hell of a gamble, my dude. You will either look like a hero or an absolute zero.'

McGuire slapped Jayce on the shoulder to return the gesture, only his wasn't so affectionate.

'Oh, believe me, it's going to be a pitch none of you will ever forget.'

Scene Four
Pitch Imperfect

McGuire had taken that wretched elevator down to the seventh floor with his four colleagues.

Whereas most people prefer to be on their own in elevators due to personal space, for McGuire it was a case of, the more the merrier. Usually, it was yet another opportunity for shenanigans. When in crowded lifts, he would often mumble things to himself under his breath, while holding the side of his head and adopt a crazed or frightened look in his eyes as he burbled out statements such as, 'No mummy, I won't kill again,' or, 'Oh my god this is just like that vision I had where we all died in an elevator crash, let me out of here, let me out of here.'

On this occasion, however, he didn't want to throw them off of their game with their impending pitches. They had clearly worked hard in preparation for today, and for him to ruin their opportunity would be beyond a dickish move. Besides, he'd have ample chance to sow his brand of disorder when he would present the final pitch at the end of the presentation.

He followed his colleagues along the corridor to a set of double doors at the far end of the floor.

Before they entered the room, Jerry cleared his throat in an effort to muster his troops' attention and give them a rallying cry.

'Okay guys, whatever happens in there, as long as you do your best and you do your ideas and your visions' justice then you've also done yourself proud, and as your manager and your friend, that's all that I can ask or expect of you. You believe in your products with a passion and vigour that's both admirable and inspiring, and as such, I believe in you guys with all of my heart. Though you don't need reminding, we're not just pitching for ourselves today, we're pitching in honour of our colleague and friend who is sadly no longer with us, and for one very special employer and friend who may not be with us for much longer. Let's go out there and give it our all and show those people in that room that Play Dates is still a brand that means something.'

The room was filled with various people in business suits, mothers with their young children, and a few employees of Play Dates - including Singer and Hensley. Undergrove was also present, breaking bread with various suited persons.

Approximately ten minutes later, Undergrove made his way to the front of the room where a lectern and microphone was placed in front of a large presentation screen connected to a laptop. Several plastic boxes had been placed below the screen, individually marked with each of the team member's names on them. For such average-sized boxes, so much hard work, dedication, and hope lay inside. There was no box present for McGuire, however. His product was being carried indignantly inside a plastic shopping bag.

Undergrove took his place behind the lectern. He had no cause to find a way to demand the room's attention, his involuntary heavy coughing along the way was more than enough of an alert.

'Good afternoon, ladies and gentlemen, mothers, fathers, and always most importantly, children. We have some new and exciting products to reveal to you today which we hope will not only make an impact on the industry in terms of sales and financial returns to you, the prospective investors, but also have a profound impact on the imagination and emotional and educational development of the children who play with them. Here at Play Dates our mantra is that we learn while we play and play while we learn, and our team, who you will meet very shortly, have embodied that ethos with their exciting new products. So, without further ado, as I'm sure the kids here, and more than likely, most of you adults too, are

keen to have a play, I introduce to you, our very own Ideas and Development team.'
A polite round of applause filled the room.
It was Jayce who was first to take the proverbial stage.

He had, by now, somewhat wisely changed from his Misfits t-shirt into a more professional attire of a slim-fit charcoal suit and cream shirt - even his vape pen had been hidden from view. He reached into the box with his name upon it behind him and pulled out what he proceeded to explain were some sensory electronic puzzle boxes. He handed some of them to the children, and then to some of the investors. He began his presentation.

What struck McGuire was the sudden change of Jayce's demeanour and vocabulary as he navigated his way through the presentation and the supporting data slides. He was eloquent, affable, and passionate.

Unfortunately, for Jayce, as impressed as the suits appeared to be with his presentation and the technical data and studies that were displayed on the screen behind him, the children in the room seemed less enamoured with the plaything - and in this room, it was the kids who held more power and importance of opinion than those writing the cheques.

A ripple of applause came from the room upon the conclusion of his presentation. Jayce's proud and heartfelt high-five to Jerry as he handed over the floor may have been misplaced in its triumph, but nonetheless, McGuire noted the sense of pride present in Jerry's eyes.

Jerry was next to take the floor. His product was another educational toy. This one was aimed at three to five-year-olds and was a battery-operated, light, colour, and sound-based gadget to develop the child's problem-solving and sensory skills. When upon repeating the correct sequence, the child would be rewarded with a tune and congratulatory message devised to build their self-esteem. Within the first ten minutes of his presentation, it was clear the children were as uninspired in their playing of the toy as his description of it. It was evident as they attempted to play it, the sequences were just too complicated for them to fully grasp and complete. If anything, they appeared to be more interested in Jerry's colourful bowtie and braces set than they were the toy he was peddling.

Tina's presentation was next.

It was hard for McGuire to get a sense of whether her pitch had been any good since it was so muffled and timid, it was hard to pick up on what was being said with any clarity. Even when the Play Dates' employee manning the sound system linked to the microphone turned up the volume on the speakers to aid not only her, but everyone else in the room, all it succeeded in doing was emphasise her frantic and nervous heavy breaths. It was as if a severe asthmatic had been let loose on an adult chat-line. If there was any saving grace to be found, at least the kids seemed entertained for a short while by the interactive action figure she had devised. Though halfway through the presentation, the children had forsaken the interactive element of the toy and were playing with it amongst their little rabble using their own voices, sayings, and actions. To them, once the interactive novelty had worn off, it was just another action figure - and the investors couldn't help but take note of this fact. Why pay additional costs for all the extra bells and whistles, when just the generic figure was all they were ultimately interested in?

Victoria was next. Not long now, then it would be McGuire's turn.

The passion she displayed for the product she was pitching was clear and infectious, and her presentation was as eloquent and as captivating as her beauty.

The product was aimed to assist the social and communication skills of those with suspected ADHD or on the spectrum. The research and data she'd presented on screen had been informative and easily digested. The data was supported by a personal story she shared about her cousin's son who had been diagnosed with Autism when they were five years old and how this product was inspired by him, and how he had been given the prototype and had shown improvements in their social awareness after playing with the toy for a prolonged period of time.

Victoria was showing a vulnerability up there which McGuire had yet to see from her cold exchanges with him, and he couldn't help but concede he was developing a bit of a crush on her, albeit a fool's one.

When opening the floor for questions from the room, Victoria was challenged by one of the potential investors about the mass market appeal of such a product. Her reply was as sincere as it was abrupt.

'I'm not presenting this for the benefit of the masses.'

The questioner seemed taken aback by this response and jotted a couple of lines in his notebook. This time, Victoria's response was not so short. She sighed heavily. She bore the look of someone who knew she was about to go off script from her well-rehearsed presentation and would hold no regrets about what she was going to say.

'I could continue to reel off the technical data that I have prepared. I can present even more of the PowerPoint slides with charts, graphs and figures that have been devised to impress you. But the bottom line is none of that really matters, does it? Data like that is just a comfort blanket for you to justify your decisions which are ultimately driven by money. Look, I get that as investors your primary responsibility is to make a profit, but here at Play Dates, our first responsibility is to the children, and it's a responsibility I'm very passionate about. Will this product be flying off the shelves at the same rate as a Transformer or a Barbie doll? No, of course not, never in a million years. Will it find itself as the first choice on children's wish lists to Santa come the season when they are subjected to the endless toy adverts that saturate the screens? No. Will you likely see a life-changing return on whatever money you may choose to invest? No. But your investment will be life-changing, and isn't that reason enough alone to want to support this? We've got a chance to do some real good here with this product, a chance to look at ourselves in the mirror and say we've helped. We're living in a world that's becoming increasingly selfish, self-obsessed, and disassociated from reality and each other. It's a world obsessed with getting validation from complete strangers who we'll never likely meet in our lives. It's a world where we're losing our humanity and humility, and it's not good enough. We can and we **should** be doing better. Will this product give these disadvantaged children an equal footing in life as those more fortunate? No. Unfortunately, it's not a magic wand. But will it help them more than if we did nothing? Of course, it will. And I guess that is all I have to say on that matter.'

McGuire looked over to Undergrove and could see the pride in his eyes. The mothers within the room as part of the focus group were also showing a look which said Girl Power was alive and strong with Victoria. The investors were harder to read. If they were stirred at all by her words they weren't letting on.

A part of McGuire felt it a shame he was about to take the attention away from what had been such a sincere moment. Yet, he had a game to play. Besides, he attempted to justify to himself. What he was about to do would make his soon-to-be ex-teammates and their products look more efficient when compared to the complete trainwreck that was about to follow.

It wasn't just showtime, it was time for a shit-show.

McGuire took to the front of the room and his position behind the lectern.

He could tell from the contrasting sets of eyes staring his way that the presentation was already expected to fail, and that was without the pandemonium he was about to unleash.

The investors in the room were weary from the preceding pitches that had failed to secure their interests.

The mothers from the focus group were exhausted from having to keep their kids in line. The children were on the verge of initiating a pint-sized revolt from not having found the marvellous and exciting new toy to play with as was promised by their parents. Finally, his team, along with Singer and Hensley, and even Sebastian Undergrove, were preparing for the worst over what would surely be a trainwreck of a ramshackle pitch. What on earth could he even be pitching other than some concepts? He'd have had no physical product to display like his teammates had. Products that had taken months to produce following the meticulous market research, focus groups and costing studies.

As McGuire cleared his throat to begin, he was resolute in not wanting to let the audience's low expectations of him go unwarranted.

'Ladies and gentlemen,' he spoke in an overly theatrical manner, reminiscent of a sports announcer announcing a boxer to their battlefield. 'Are you ready to rock?'

McGuire followed this statement by pulling out a party popper he had acquired from a pound shop and pulled the string, releasing an impotent sounding bang followed by an underwhelming amount of paper streamers shooting into the air.

'Sorry,' he then followed in an apologetic tone. 'I wanted some pyros and a laser show for my introduction, but due to health and safety and logistical reasons, I had to use these party poppers instead.' His explanation was delivered with such a lack of humour and irony that it only served to cause confusion amongst the room. He then pulled out another party popper and let if off with a bitter expression on his face.

He allowed a long enough pause for the silence to become uncomfortable, before beginning to speak again.

'Good afternoon, ladies, gentlemen, and children,' he began innocuously enough. 'Mr Potato Head is an iconic toy. Adored by generations for seventy years. He was even immortalised on screen by the Toy Story franchise. Mr Potato Head is simplistic in its design, high in sales revenue, low on production costs, and decidedly licensable with its scope for various accessories. Today, I'm here to pitch to you, a new food-inspired toy that will bring great delight and hours of fun to the next generation of consumers. I'm here to introduce you to, Krayzie Cucumber - and you know he's crazy because it's spelled wrong and begins with a K. And what's cooler to kids these days than unapologetic illiteracy? Why is he so Krayzie, you may rightly ask? Well, please allow me to show you.'

McGuire remained stone-faced as he pulled out what was blatantly a large, green, vibrating sex toy from his bag. He didn't even break into a smile when the aghast gasps came from every direction of the room.

'Just like Mr Potato Head, you'll be able to add accessories to pimp him up how you see fit.'

McGuire pulled out a pack of stickable googly eyes he had also acquired from the pound shop, along with a sticker of a mouth, and stuck them onto the vibrator. He then pulled out some craft pipe cleaner and manufactured a pair of arms by wrapping it around the phallic toy. He then turned it on, causing the googly eyes to start rolling.

One of the young children came up to the lectern giggling. Her arms were reached out in a gesture that suggested she wanted to play with it. McGuire was only too pleased to oblige. He was able to hand the vibrator to the child before her mortified mother could stop him.

To most of the room's dismay - and McGuire's delight - the child then began to chase some of the other children around the room with it laughing and yelling.

'Krayzie Cucumber, Krayzie Cucumber.'

McGuire reached into his bag and pulled out another party popper and unenthusiastically let it off. Still, McGuire refused to break character and began to recite some technical info in a deadpan manner.

'This is just a prototype of course, there are still a few minor design tweaks to iron out, but the recommended retail price will be £19.99, a five hundred percent increase of its production cost, plus it's easy to wipe clean and contains no choking hazards. For the girls, it will also be available in pink.'

McGuire reached into the shopping bag and pulled out a pink vibrator with the googly eyes and mouth pre-stuck to it.

There were tears coming from the kids in the room now. Though not because they didn't like the product. One mortified mother was trying desperately to pry the vibrator from her child's hand. Some of the other mothers were dragging their children kicking and screaming from the room, leaving in an outraged haste. Some of the advertisers had seen enough too - or in this case, they had seen far too much. They also left in outrage.

McGuire looked over proudly to his team and could see their stunned expressions, Jerry was literally open-mouthed in shock over what he had just witnessed. Tina was visibly shaken, Victoria's familiar look of contempt towards him had returned with a vengeance, and even Sebastian Undergrove was left dumbfounded.

McGuire felt glorious.

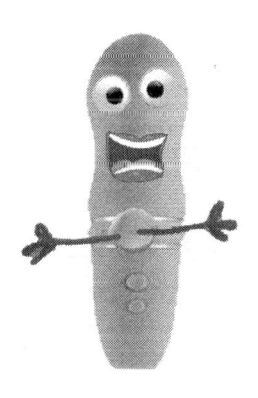

Scene Five
Radio Daze

Even the Play Dates jingle didn't sound as irritating to McGuire as he joined his soon-to-be-former teammates in the elevator back to their office. To inflict further aggravation upon them, he even began singing the ditty in an overly enthusiastic manner.

If looks could kill, then he wouldn't have been the subject of a whodunnit book, but instead a, how-many-of-them-dunnit.

'Dude,' Jayce spoke to McGuire as he walked with him back to his desk. 'If you're not careful, you're going to get yourself fired. Seriously, I've known Jerry for a couple of years now and I've never seen him this pissed off at someone for that shit you pulled back there in that presentation.'

McGuire gave himself a mental high five.

'I've got to tell you man,' Jayce continued, 'If it was up to Jerry, he'd sack you right here on the spot.'

McGuire's mental high-fiving turned limp.

'What do you mean, if it was up to Jerry?'

'Undergrove gets the final say over who gets fired. After what happened to Niles when Jerry let him go, he wanted it to be so that responsibility was his and his alone, just in case of any other unfortunate repercussions. That way, it would only be his own burden and conscience which had to deal with any guilt. When he goes, which doesn't sound like it will be long, whoever takes over this company is going to have some special shoes to fill, that's for sure.'

McGuire slumped in his chair. This was not the news he wanted to hear.

Undergrove had clearly gone to bat for him and was already showing a real soft spot towards him. His confidence in getting fired over his performance at the presentation was not as infallible as it had been before. The only types of people who would keep him around after this afternoon's antics would be the world's biggest idiots or the world's biggest sweethearts, and Undergrove weighed heavy on the sweetie scale.

'Hey Barry,' Jerry spoke. His voice was lacking the affability which had previously been shown towards him. 'For the rest of the day, I want you to complete your on-line induction course. There's not much you need to do other than watch the videos.' He then added in an uncharacteristic passive-aggressive tone. 'Not even you can cause chaos doing that.'

'Challenge accepted,' McGuire spoke in his mind. It was obvious to him that Jerry was trying to clip his wings and restrain him as much as he could until he'd had a chance to speak to Undergrove about his future in the team. It was a solid enough tactic, but not one that McGuire hadn't been on the receiving end of before.

Upon logging into his PC with the details provided, McGuire was quick to test the company's I.T controls.

As he had anticipated for such a family-friendly organisation, he was instantly thwarted by the internet displaying a web blocker blocking social media, gambling, and adult entertainment sites - in other words, all the stuff that makes the internet worthwhile.

'Hey Jerry,' he shouted from across the office, purposely loud enough for everyone else to hear. 'Is there any way I can bypass the internet's site blocker? This is a bit embarrassing for me to say aloud, especially with it being my first day, and us only just becoming such good friends and everything, but I get the sense that you aren't the judgemental sort. For full disclosure, I have a bit of an addiction to Internet Porn. Ever since I was about seven years old in fact. Long story short, I've seen so much freaky stuff online over the years, the only thing that does anything for me in the trouser department these days is the stuff on the dark web. Don't worry, I'm not some kind of nonce, I don't go for anything illegal. The older the better in my eyes - if you catch my drift. Anyways, I've recently gotten myself into Amputee Midget Clown porn and found a site that is second to none in providing that kind of content.'

Jerry wasn't biting.

'Just follow the instructions I've given you Barry,' he sighed. 'And please remember to be appropriate in the workplace. Otherwise, I'll have no choice but to make a formal complaint to H.R.'

'No problemo boss,' he replied unperturbed. 'Sorry. Won't bring it up again.'

He looked around the room to observe the reaction of his colleagues and could see Tina making the sign of the Christian cross to him in the air as if she believed he was the devil himself, shat out from the asshole of hell.

McGuire remained silent for a few minutes and had even started the online orientation course to allow a false sense of calm to rebuild before letting loose with his next attempt. Then their reprieve ended.

'Do you guys have a radio or anything for some background noise? The atmosphere's a bit tense in here for some unknown reason and it's bringing my vibe down.'

'No Barry,' Jerry groaned. 'We don't have a radio.'

'That's quite alright,' McGuire replied. 'I've brought my magic radio with me to listen to.'

McGuire channelled his inner mime artist and mimicked pulling out a radio from the drawer and placed it on his desk.

'It's a bit of an antique,' he spoke to Jayce who was looking at him dumbfounded. 'It's not like those MP3 players, or whatever it is you kids are down with these days. It's an analogue. Hopefully, I can get a good reception here.' He began twisting some imaginary dials for a few seconds, even making some swishing noises with his mouth to mimic the static. 'Ah, here we go. Radio One.' McGuire then began beatboxing a hip-hop beat.

'Can't go wrong with some NWA,' he commented before resuming his beats and bursting into some rap that was clearly more WTF than NWA.

'Barry, will you stop!' Jerry commanded, clearly having his patience worn thin by this unwelcome team member.

'Hang on,' Barry replied. 'Let me just turn the radio down.' McGuire twisted some more imaginary buttons. 'Sorry, boss, what did you say?'

'I said will you stop!'

'Ah okay, my bad, that was inconsiderate of me. I should have asked what you guys wanted first. Would you prefer Radio 2 instead?'

'I'd prefer you to shut the hell up,' the abrupt response came, much to McGuire's secret delight.

Scene Six
Some You Win, Summons You Lose

The hour was coming up to half four - almost time for McGuire's first day to come to an end.

This time of the working day was largely unfamiliar territory for him. He only had half an hour remaining to get his employment terminated on the first day.

Jerry's phone began to ring and was answered promptly before the second ring could even complete its cycle.

'Jerry speaking.' There was a minor pause. 'Oh, hi Bastian.'

McGuire noticed that Jerry's eye line instinctively turned towards him, then quickly turned away as their eyes met. It was clear that whatever was being said on the other end of the line, he was the subject of the one-sided conversation, and judging from Jerry's avoidance of eye contact, it wasn't likely to be a favourable topic.

'Okie Dokey,' Jerry spoke. 'I'll send him over to you right away.'

McGuire's suspicions had been confirmed, he'd even stood up already and had started his move.

'Barry,' Jerry spoke. 'Mr Undergrove would like you to go and see him in his office as soon as possible please.'

'Sure thing,' he gladly spoke.

Scene Seven
Schlock and Awe

'Come in Barry,' Undergrove spoke upon hearing the knock at the door. He didn't even need McGuire to introduce himself. He was expected.

He entered Undergrove's office and was quick to observe a male, aged in their early-fifties, stood in the room. The stranger was dressed in an expensive-looking black suit and wasn't familiar to McGuire. He suspected he was a representative from the HR department.

'Quite the first day you've had,' Undergrove spoke before letting out one of his trademark hefty splutters into a handkerchief. 'You certainly know how to make an impression.'

'Well, a lion who roars too soon may startle its pray and go without its meal for a while, but it's presence has been heard by all on the plain, and now they know it's hungry.'

'I've not heard that saying before, but if truth be told, I am still undecided whether you are a lion or just a jackass. One thing I do know, however, is that you defy conventional logic. Your antics alone in your presentation earlier should have been enough to see you fired, and until about half an hour ago, I was ready to make that difficult decision to let you go. I was going to cut my losses and put it down as a lesson learnt that my decision to take a gamble on you was one that simply didn't pay off.'

McGuire didn't like the way in which Undergrove was referring to wanting to fire him as past tense.

Undergrove continued.

'I'd like to introduce you to Solomon Wright. Solomon was one of the potential investors present at the pitches today.'

The stranger who had now been introduced as someone not from HR, but as an investor, extended their hand for McGuire to shake.

'It's great to meet you Barry,' Solomon greeted. 'I've got to say, I've seen some pitches in my time, but none as memorable as that one. You've got raw talent, my friend. I'd love to invest in your product, more importantly, I want to invest in you.'

As much as McGuire fancied himself as a master of the poker face, even he couldn't help but hide his astonishment at this news.

'I can see you are almost as surprised as I was,' Undergrove laughed. 'I mean, granted there were a large number of the invited guests that were outraged. So much so, I've literally had to spend most of the time since the presentation ended on phone calls apologising to guests and parents for the inappropriateness of what they had to witness. But then Solomon came by the office and told me the good news.'

'Your product still needs some tweaks to the design for obvious reasons,' Solomon continued. 'But Sebastian explained that you literally had a few hours to come up with that product, which makes it even more remarkable. If that's what you can come up with in a few hours on your very first day here, I'm excited to see what you can come up with when you have more time to prepare. In all the years I've been investing in children's products, I'd be hard pressed to remember a time where I've seen the children of a focus group be that excited over a toy, and if it's good enough for them, then it's good enough for me.'

Undergrove reached into a drawer and pulled out a party popper and let it off. He had a huge smile etched into his face.

This had to be some sick joke. Maybe Undergrove and this Solomon person were messing with his head and providing him with a taste of his own medicine before giving him his marching orders.

'The workday's almost over Barry, why don't you take an early finish?' Undergrove added. 'Tomorrow, the hard work begins.'

Solomon gave McGuire a hearty handshake. Undergrove's was less sturdy, as moments later, he began another coughing fit and waved McGuire out.

Scene Eight
In Need of a Lift

With the time 16:45, McGuire made his way to the stairwell. The eight flights of stairs may have been more of a physical hindrance than the elevator, but not having to listen to that excruciating Play Dates jingle again was a sacrifice more than worth it.

If there was any lingering doubt in his mind that today was one of those days, if Karma existed, she was collecting a down payment with added interest for all the rotten things McGuire had done during his playing of the game.

The stairway was blocked off by some maintenance workers fixing some lighting hanging from one of the ceiling panels.

'Sorry buddy,' the worker supporting the ladder spoke as he saw McGuire's approach. 'You'll have to take one of the lifts. Unless you want to wait for half an hour.'

The decision wasn't as easy for McGuire as the worker expected it to be. He clearly hadn't been subjected to the crime against music that was the Play Dates ditty.

Begrudgingly McGuire conceded that the lift would be the best option. The commute home was long enough as it was, and should he miss the next train, it would cause a domino effect of missed connections and increasing frustration. The lyrics to an Elvis Presley song sprang immediately to mind.

When nothin' is right
From mornin' to night
Didja' ever get one of them days, boy.

At least it was a far more favourable tune than the one inside the elevator it was fated to be replaced by.

He trudged back to the foyer and pressed the down button on the wall panel in between the two elevators.

The doors to the right-hand side elevator opened and McGuire stepped into it.

He was about to press the button for the ground floor when he saw a man aged in his early forties in a sand-coloured suit, standing in front of the open doors.

Despite the well-tailored suit, it wasn't enough to distract from its owner's dishevelled look. His salt and pepper hair was unkempt, and the wild stubble upon his face suggested that he hadn't shaved for a week or so. Plus, there was the stench of liquor exuding from him. It would seem to McGuire that he wasn't the only one having a bad day at the office.

Reluctantly, McGuire pressed the button for the doors to stay open to allow this man to get in. The stranger said nothing. He just stared at McGuire through his bloodshot eyes. McGuire presumed it had either been from drinking or crying, possibly even both. Either way, McGuire began to feel like it would be himself having to endure an elevator nutter. Karma was taking yet another down payment from him.

'Are you getting in or not mate?' McGuire questioned as he pre-emptively pressed the button to keep the doors open again.

Still, the man said nothing. He just continued to stare penetratingly.

'Last chance buddy.'

The man remained silent but appeared to mouth something which McGuire couldn't decipher.

The elevator doors closed. This time, McGuire wasn't feeling Samaritan enough to keep them open. He instead pressed the button to go to the ground floor.

With his focus taken away from that frayed-looking man, the Play Dates ditty took full advantage of the moment and invaded his ears and mind yet again. Then it happened. The elevator jolted and came to an abrupt halt, almost rocking him off his feet.

'You've got to be shitting me,' McGuire cussed. 'Could this day get any worse?'

He pressed a few buttons frantically as if he was playing

an old beat em up video game in an attempt to get it moving again. There was no response.

Any consolation that at least the electrics were still working were negated by the fact that it also meant the sound system was still working, and that meant the Play Dates jingle was still playing on loop. Fuck you, Karma.

He pressed the emergency alarm on the side panel. A voice came from the intercom.

'Good evening, you are through to the dedicated emergency monitoring service this is Mike, can I confirm this call has not been initiated in error please.'

'No, Mike, I like being stuck in a lift with this fucking Godawful song being played on loop.'

'Oh yeah, is that the Play Dates song? I remember that from when I was a kid. Wow, I didn't even realise they were still around.'

'Yup, and I'm stuck in one of their lifts at their head office.'

'Okay pal, just sit tight. I'll notify our emergency technicians now and they'll get with you as soon as they can. I've got the address from your emergency alarm code. Can I confirm with you please if you have any medical conditions that may require any extra assistance?'

'Well, I have developed a major pain in the ass since starting this job.

'Hah, very good pal. Well, just sit tight and a technician will be with you as soon as they can. Hopefully, the traffic won't be too bad. If you begin to develop any medical emergencies, please call 999.'

Close to an hour had passed before McGuire was finally freed from the elevator.

'Sorry guvner,' the technician called out to him in a cockney accent, which even Dick van Dyke in Mary Poppins would have found laid on too thick. 'There was a traffic accident causing a jam and stopping us from getting here sooner. This elevator's been a pain in the ass for us lately. It's the third time already this month it's packed in.

Most people tend to avoid using it now and just use the other one instead. Ah well, you're out now, that's what matters.'

Scene Nine
The Fallow Formula

It was gone 23:00 by the time McGuire finally made it home.

He opened the door and slumped himself down on the sofa with all the delicateness of someone dropping a sandbag. He couldn't even find the motivation to lift himself back up to go to the fridge and pull out the ice-cold beer he'd had a hankering for. At least he'd managed to pick up some food between his connections, or at least the railway station's interpretation of food – twice the price, half the taste. All he wanted to do now was crash out until he had to be up early again the following morning. He hated nights like these where he felt they had been wasted.

His thoughts returned for the second time this day to his late foster brother, Joseph. As bad as a day it had been for McGuire, he pushed himself to remember that his brother felt like it was, 'one of those days,' every day for a sustained period.

Like McGuire, Joseph had been a scholar, and had graduated from university with a bachelor's degree in economics. He'd had a zest for life, and a spark in his eyes that shone brightly.

Unlike, his little brother, following his graduation, Joseph had walked into his dream job. That role was as a Stockbroker – the 50p DVD he had found of The Wolf of Wall Street in their local charity shop had a lot to answer for.

It had been during the last few months of McGuire's degree that he received the call informing him of his brother's self-inflicted passing. Never did McGuire realise that a one-minute call from a complete stranger would change the course of his life's direction, and his perspective on it, for however long forever actually lasts.

For a while, as was natural, McGuire began to question if he was to blame. The warning signs had been there for him to see. On the increasingly rare occasions that he managed to meet up with Joey, he was becoming more of a stranger to him each time. He was uncharacteristically distant, and the fire in his eyes had been turned down to a gentle simmer. He was no longer a hot pot of dreams and ambition, but a Pot Noodle of going through the motions with minimal effort.

What struck McGuire, upon his pained reflection, was Joey's talk of work. It was filled with a quiet, almost menacing, disdain. The more he thought of it, the more he likened it to a pulp fiction murder mystery, where the victim was giving the intrepid hero of the story the cryptic clues of their killer's identity before the deed was actually committed. As he began to dissect the murder scene ala CSI Chelmsley Green, the reveal of the thrilling finale placed the murderer's identity as, work. The time of death, anywhere between the hours of 9-5.

As he pieced together all of his brother's comments relating to the adverse effects that his work was getting in the way of his life, McGuire had come up with something he liked to call the Fallow Formula. The conclusion of his calculations was that there just weren't enough hours in the day to fully live your life and be completely free from the working day at the same time.

The calculation is as follows and is based on the average job being between the hours of working 9-5, as confirmed by the sage-like wisdom of Dolly Parton.

If you add in the variable of the sixty-minute commute each way (factoring in traffic or walking to the public transport location) the time the job is now taking out of your life now becomes 8-6. Don't blame Dolly for this glaring omission in her catchy little tune, however. Working Eight til Six just hasn't got the same ring to it.

The formula doesn't stop here though as you must factor in the additional forces of opposition to the timings.

On average, you would need to get up, thirty minutes to an hour earlier in order to have breakfast, along with the time needed to shit, shower (and depending on gender and follicle preference) have a shave too.

All of a sudden, the hours between 8-6 that your commitment to work has taken from your life has now become 7-6.

Then the formula takes into account your returning home from the working day. It is now time for your evening meal, and unless you're a heathen living their life on frozen microwave meals, another hour can be added onto this time for cooking, eating, and dishwashing commitments. Suddenly, you've given any uninterrupted downtime between the hours of 07:00 and 19:00 a big sloppy kiss goodbye.

The calculations don't end there, however. Not without the external factors that also need to be added into this equation. These include elements such as friends, family, or significant others.

Upon your social visits with afore mention friends, family, or significant others, one of the conversations that will inevitably come up will be about how your day has been. So now, not only have you spent most of said time revolving around your working day, but you are now having to make small talk about it in your free time too. Half an hour extra on average can be chalked up to this conversation, but also, unless your social skills are lacking and borderline sociopathic, it is only right that you reciprocate the question and ask how their day has been too. This now means that invariably, you not only have to talk about your own job outside of working hours but also have to listen to someone else talk about theirs too. Let's call this another average of half an hour, and for clarification, that's not even taking into consideration any work nights out where inevitably, seventy percent of conversations include work, and in this instance, you're not only spending drinking money on talking work, but you're going to wake up with a hangover to show for it. Anyway, that's a whole different equation, let's get back to the Fallow Formula. It's now the hours of 07:00 and 20:00 of your day gone directly or indirectly due to work, despite only being paid for only almost half of that time.

Exhausted yet?

Funnily you should say that, as now you have sleep to add into the equation. It is recommended that an adult needs on average between seven and nine hours of sleep a day. So, if you deduct the median of eight hours from the seven o'clock you need to wake up for the following day, you're looking at an eleven O'clock bedtime. This would then leave you with an average of three hours a day of uninterrupted respite time not spent related directly or indirectly to work.

Scene Ten
Dog Tired

McGuire's eyes began to feel heavy upon the sofa as the tiredness was proving too powerful an adversary to fight. He forced himself from the sofa in one final act of defiance against the inevitable sleep and made his way to the greater comfort of his bed. By half past eleven McGuire was in a deep slumber and would stay that way until 05:15 the following morning.

He didn't even hear the sounds of a large and fierce dog coming from downstairs, set off by the motion sensors inside the front door.

Part Five

Day Two

Scene One
Destined for Lateness

McGuire's retro, radio alarm clock sprang into action at the unfavourable time of 05:15.

The first disagreeable thing that struck McGuire as he was woken by the sound of Bill Withers' deluded declaration that it was "gonna be a lovely day," wasn't the earliness of the hour, but an overwhelming stench invading his sinuses. It was the smell of what he was sure was animal urine, though, what type of animal it was, he couldn't be certain.

Somehow, something had gotten into his home.

He followed the pungent smell along the landing and towards the spare room. The door to the room was closed, as he had expected it to be.

He wondered if maybe he had left the spare room window open and a cat, or maybe even a fox, had managed to climb up and crawl through for whatever reason. Yet the sight that greeted him, once he had opened the door, was not one he had anticipated.

The ammonia aroma was even more concentrated once inside the room, yet this was not the cause for his most concern. Papers and stationery from on top his desk had been scattered about the place, and in some instances torn.

His eyes veered towards the window to see that it was closed.

'Rats,' he muttered aloud. Both as a curse word and as an accusation. 'They must have gotten through the wall somehow,' he reasoned further.

He would have to call the landlord later, but for now his immediate concern was disinfecting the room and getting rid of that potent stench. It would undoubtedly push him behind on his travel schedule to get to the office on time, but what was the worst they could do to, fire him?

The idea of turning up late wasn't one that McGuire favoured. For all his flaws, punctuality was never one of them. Besides, if he was to get fired for something outside of his control, the dismissal wouldn't count towards his game stats.

Though McGuire had never been a believer of fate, today was one of those occasions where he knew he was destined for lateness.

To add further delays to that caused by his scrubbing everything he could in the spare room with bleach, the next train was pronounced as running late due to what the platform announcement declared to be a mechanical failure. The knock-on effect caused by these delays would likely see him arrive at least two hours behind his contracted start time.

He had already called through at nine o'clock on the number provided in the employee handbook for such occasions and had been redirected to Jerry's number.

Upon reaching his manager, he even sensed a tone of relief in Jerry's voice upon his declaration that he wouldn't be arriving until likely after eleven o'clock.

'Well, just see what time you get here. Don't feel you need to rush.' This last part was spoken in more of an order than a pleasantry.

Not to be perturbed by being deemed temporarily out of action by being stuck on a train, it was time for McGuire to get proactive. After all, is that not one of the qualities most employers say they are looking for?

'Ideas and Development Team, Jerry speaking,' the

polite and enthusiastic answer came as McGuire rang through to him directly this time. It was five minutes past nine.

'Jerry, it's Barry. I just thought I'd call and give you another update. I'm still going to be late but at least I'm on the train now.'

'That's fine Barry, thank you for keeping me in the loop, I'll see you when you get in.'

Jerry hung up the phone, only for it to ring a few minutes later.

'Ideas and Development Team. Jerry speaking.' His tone was still polite and enthusiastic. McGuire sensed it wouldn't be long before that would change.

'Hi Jerry, it's Barry. I forgot to tell you something on our last phone call. I had a dream about you last night. You were half man, half stallion, and I was dressed as a Roman Gladiator riding you into battle. It was glorious.'

'Please only call this number for work-related issues Barry.'

Jerry hung up again, though this time not without letting loose with a heavy sigh. He had inadvertently shown weakness to McGuire.

A few more minutes passed.

The phone rang again.

'Ideas and Development Team, Jerry speaking.' This time, though courteous, the tone wasn't so enthusiastic.

'Jerry, it's Barry. Still on the train. Just calling to let you know that I've just had a coffee and a cereal bar from the buffet cart. I thought I'd best let you know. Just in case you were worried about any potential dehydration and low sugar levels I may suffer on my journey. They're silent killers you know.'

'I'm glad you're going to live, Barry. I'm very busy, please stop calling me.'

The phone was slammed down with more of anger than frustration this time.

A mere two minutes of silence passed before Jerry's phone rang yet again.

'For the love of god, will you stop fucking calling me.'

'Jerry!' the weakened voice came, followed by some heavy coughing. 'Is that an appropriate way to answer the work phone?'

'Sebastian! I'm so sorry, I thought it was…er, never mind. Is everything okay?'

'Apart from my concerns over your phone etiquette, everything is fine Jerry. I just phoned to see if you wanted to come to my office for a debrief over yesterday's presentations.'

'Sure thing, I'll be over now.'

Scene Two
Unwelcome Committee

The time was a little past quarter to eleven by the time McGuire cantered into the Ideas and Development office. He could see by the maddened eyes that met his arrival that his presence in the office was as welcome as a haemophiliac in an acupuncture clinic.

In the few years since beginning his game, he had grown used to the galled gazes of his colleagues. They would frequently entail a blend of befuddlement, infuriation, rage, despair, and on occasion, even pity. This collection of looks being volleyed his way, however, were not ones he could remember seeing before. These were looks of resentment.

McGuire quickly, and accurately, deduced that news of his abomination of a so-called product being picked up to go to market had reached his team. He also correctly concluded by their antipathy towards him that none of their products had been afforded such a result.

McGuire felt genuine regret that none of their products had been chosen to go forward to the manufacturing stage, especially Victorias'. Unlike himself, they had actually put in the hard work and cared about their creations. Alas, empathy was not a trait that playing this game favoured.

'Did someone fart or something?' he crassly joked, purposely misreading the room.

'The only thing that is lingering and unwelcome with its foul presence is you,' Victoria spoke curtly.

Even when she was berating him with such aplomb it was hard for McGuire to deny her beauty.

'Now, now, Victoria,' Jerry attempted to defuse. 'Let's try and keep our emotions and opinions in check before something gets said that the HR department would take an active interest in.'

'So, this imbecile gets to wave a sex toy at some

children and gets rewarded for it. I say what everyone in this room is thinking and I get chided. I thought that this was the company where the only opinion that mattered was an honest one.'

Jerry let out a huge sigh that suggested he would rather be any place else in the world right now than the burgeoning battlefield that was his office.

'Barry,' he then followed. 'Sebastian wants to see you in his office. As soon as you can, please.'

Scene Three
The Third Degree of Separation

'Barry, you finally made it in,' Undergrove spoke as McGuire entered his office and took a seat opposite him at the desk.

There was no snideness present in Undergrove's tone as he referenced his lateness.

'Jerry kept me in the loop about you running late. Though, not as much as you elected to keep him updated, it would seem. In all the years I have known Jerry, I have never known anyone to get under his skin as much as you have managed to in just one day. I would put it down to him not sharing the same sense of humour as you do, but alas, I don't think that statement can only be limited to just him. As I've always said, Barry. The only opinion that matters here is an honest one, and as such, I'm going to have to be blunt with you.'

McGuire noticed a seriousness in Undergrove's voice that hadn't been directed his way previously.

'You haven't exactly enamoured yourself with your new team mates thus far. From the feedback I've received about your first day with them, they've found you to be crass, obnoxious, shameless, vulgar, and inconsiderate. And these are the more favourable terms lobbied your way. Team spirit is something we pride ourselves upon in this company, and resentment and squabbles in the workplace have a way of escalating into something far more toxic, and I won't abide that here. As such, it's left me no option but to separate you from them.'

McGuire threw Undergrove an inadvertent look of confusion.

'Separate us how exactly?'

'We have an office going spare which you can now use as your own. I'll put a call through to the IT department to get you set up there. Don't look at it as a punishment, most people would love to have their own office. And it's not as if you'll be a leper or a pariah, my door is always open to you Barry.'

Scene Four
The Truce of the Matter

McGuire was in a lousy mood as he sat behind the desk in his new office - if it could even be called that.

Judging by the mountains of stationery boxes and printer paper surrounding the desk, it was clear that this room's main use these days was as an ad-hoc storeroom, and McGuire had been relocated here like the rest of the surplus stock.

A sense of déjà vu of days long past came over him as he recalled the occasions where he had been sentenced to school detention and had the classroom all to himself with nothing else to do other than stare the clock down until he could rejoin the masses. His proverbial wings had been well and truly clipped, he was no longer an exceptional eagle soaring high, but an ostracised ostrich unable to take flight. He still hadn't even a PC delivered to his new desk.

The irony had not been lost upon him that he was actually willing to do some work just to pass some time away. Even those worthless on-line legislation courses he had been tasked with completing yesterday seemed as enticing as a big-screen summer blockbuster movie.

Never one to be defeated, McGuire decreed to make some good use of this free time by brainstorming a battle plan going forward. They may have exiled him to this office, but it wasn't as if he was chained to the desk. He was free to wander around the building and there were loads of different offices for him to visit and people to torment to unleash his brand of chaos. First things first, however, he needed to see if the rat problem back home had been sorted.

'Hello,' the chirpy male voice came from the other end of the line after McGuire had dialled his landlord's number.

'Hi Mr Fallon, it's Barry McGuire from number 82

Birchwood. I called earlier about a possible rat problem.'

'Ah yes,' the reply came. 'Funnily enough, I've just come from there with the pest controller and was about to ring you. We had a good look around the place and couldn't see any traces of rodents at all.'

'But what about that strong stench of urine and the papers that were destroyed in the spare room?'

'We couldn't smell anything like that in there.'

'Maybe because I disinfected the place before I left this morning. I was pretty thorough.'

'Not thorough enough it would seem Barry.'

'I'm not sure I follow. I thought you said you couldn't smell anything in there.'

'I said we couldn't smell anything like, rat piss. What we could smell was stale alcohol, it smelt like a distillery in there. My educated guess is that you had an almighty bender last night. You probably destroyed some of your things and pissed in the room somewhere, not remembered anything about it and blamed it on some rats when you woke up. Hey, I'm not judging you, we all need to let loose sometimes, and as long as you're not doing anything illegal then you can unwind any old way you like. And aside from it smelling like a brewery in there, the house was very well kept and clean. So as long as you keep paying your rent on time, we're all good.'

'No, that can't be right,' McGuire defensively defied. 'I didn't even have a drink last night. I didn't get back from work until very late and then I just went straight to bed.'

'Working late, Barry!' Fallon laughed. 'Are you sure you're not still drunk? The infamous Fire McGuire, who's barely managed to work a full day in his life! Catch you soon mate.'

The phone call ended leaving McGuire perplexed. Why his landlord would concoct a story about the place smelling of alcohol was beyond him. Maybe he hadn't gone out on that visit with the pest controller at all and was just finding a way to cover his tracks.

There was to be no respite from his bafflement as almost as soon as the puzzling phone call was ended, there was a gentle knock on his office door. McGuire presumed it was the IT guys bringing his computer equipment to set up at long last. He summoned them in yet was amazed to see it was Victoria who entered instead. She looked almost as coy as her knock on the door.

'Hi there, I've come to apologise to you for the things I said earlier. It wasn't very professional of me, and above all, well, it just wasn't very nice.'

McGuire couldn't help but let out a smile of disbelief. 'What the hell is wrong with this place?' He thought. 'I've acted almost exclusively like a prick to my teammates, yet still it's one of them who comes forward with an apology instead. It's as though I've taken one giant leap into a Twilight Zone episode.'

'Hey, don't sweat it,' he spoke amiably to show there was genuinely no hard feelings. If she only knew the truth about some of the other things he'd been called during his time playing this game, then perhaps her only regret over what was said was that she didn't go far enough. 'You didn't say anything to me that wasn't true,' McGuire returned.

He could see Victoria was struggling with her pride to come and see him, and he wasn't about to shovel further shit upon her whilst she was down.

'Even so, it wasn't the right thing to do. I was more frustrated that my product got passed over for yours. There was more than a hint of jealousy and bitterness that caused my outburst. And that's on me, not you.'

She made an improvised seat out of the stacked boxes of printer paper and sat down on it. Her feet didn't even touch the floor from her makeshift chair. McGuire noted in his mind that all she needed was a fishing rod in her hands and she'd double for one of those garden gnome ornaments. He shared this observation with her, and she let out a gentle and sincere smile.

'I can see why Sebastian likes you,' she said. 'He doesn't smile so much these days for obvious reasons, but you seem to bring out the child in him. I think he thought that side of things had been eaten away by that awful cancer of his.' Her solemn tone at this statement turned to one more fun-natured with her next. 'I still think you're a cunt though.'

McGuire let out a belly laugh upon hearing this.

'Whoah, do you kiss your mother with that mouth? This is one of the most insulting apologies I think I've ever heard. I like it. And for what it's worth, I don't blame you for being pissed at me for them choosing to go forward with my product. I was taking the piss up there for some shits and giggles, never in a million years did I think some investor would actually like my idea.'

'Well, you know what they say, a fool and their money are soon parted.'

'You guys say honesty is the only opinion that matters in this place, right?' McGuire stated.

She nodded her head.

'I think those money people are idiots for not picking up your idea.'

'Well, if we're playing truth tennis, let me throw another volley at you. I have a bit of an agenda for coming to see you.'

'You mean coming in here to call me a c-word wasn't your main intention? Grab your crayons and colour me intrigued.'

'Sebastian asked me if I could work with you, to help you with the more technical aspects of your product, since he's aware you have no experience in that side of things. He seems to think I'd keep you in line and bring out the best of you better than anyone else on the team would. Jaycon would be too impressionable, Tina would have a breakdown, and Jerry just straight out detests you. I told Sebastian I'd think about it.'

'Because you think I'm a c-word?'

'Amongst other reasons. This is where it comes down to my hidden agenda. I think I have a way of subtly combining my product with yours so that it can achieve some of the same things as my idea did.'

'Kinda like a Trojan Horse, you mean. Get your product to market under a different guise, right under the investor's nose.'

'It's a win-win situation, and you said it yourself, you think those guys are idiots for not picking it up.'

McGuire let out a heavy sigh.

'I don't think that's a good idea.'

He saw Victoria's face stiffen; she was trying hard to fight displaying her disappointment. It was a look he found hard to resist.

'I didn't mean for it to come out like that. The idea itself is great. So much so, that on the buffet cart of great ideas it's the equivalent of a chicken drumstick as opposed to a celery stick. What I meant to say is that I am not the right person you want to be collaborating with. Not sure if you noticed or not, but I'm not exactly Mr Reliable. Even Freddy Krueger is a safer pair of hands than I am.'

'Which is another of my reasons for telling Sebastian that I'll think about teaming with you. Look, I'm not an idiot. I can see you're trying to get yourself fired from here. I don't know why you're going through all that effort when you could just simply quit, but quite frankly, that's your business, not mine. What I will say though, unless you do something so unbelievably heinous, it's not going to happen. People don't get fired from this place anymore. Not as long as Sebastian is around. Not after what happened to Niles.'

'I heard about that. I also heard you two were…close. For what it's worth, I know exactly what you're going through, and I'm sorry.'

'Someone's empathy is always worth something in this world, so thank you. This company and his job meant the world to him. I think that's why he took the failure of his last product so hard when it did so poorly in the market. He was a very sensitive soul, even at the best of times. Things just started to get away from him and snowball after that. Believe it or not, this was his office for a while.

Jerry was finding it harder and harder to cover for Niles as his drinking was starting to affect his performance, which meant Sebastian was starting to take notice too. He was starting to put pressure on Jerry to get it sorted. As much as Jerry is a good man, unfortunately, he's not so strong when it comes to conflict. For him, sorting it meant the out of sight and out of mind approach in the hope that Niles would get better on his own accord. We all agreed we'd pick up the extra workload between us until things with him improved. I'd come in and check on him of course, how could I not? He was very dear to me. But the changes in him were getting to be even more noticeable. I wouldn't class him as an angry person when he drank per se, but he was certainly getting to be more agitated and erratic. He'd go on rants at me about how this place was his lifeblood and if anybody ever did anything to hurt this business, or anyone he cared about inside it, then he wouldn't be responsible for his actions. Some of his other rants were so incoherent they would make very little sense. For the first time since I'd met him, I wasn't feeling comfortable around him. It just wasn't Niles anymore. That's when I told him until he sorted his life out, I wanted nothing to do with him. Those were the last words I said to him before Jerry finally had no choice but to let him go. Thinking about it, this is the first time I've been in this office since he…well, you know.'

Victoria wiped the tears from her eyes with the sleeve of her top.

'Jees. I think I preferred our conversations when you were insulting me.' McGuire attempted to soothe.

'I'm sorry, I didn't mean to throw so much on you. We don't really talk about what happened, it's kind of our dirty little secret here.'

McGuire was about to say something, but both their hearts jumped at the sound of a pigeon hitting the office window. So hard was the impact, a stain of blood and other clotted matter remained in place from the point of collision.

'Well, that's a metaphor about how my day's been going so far,' McGuire joked once his sense of calm had reset.

Victoria let out another gentle smile.

'I'm glad we had this talk, Barry. It's helped me with my decision. I think I **can** be able to work with you.'

'You're not worried over the fact that I could be fired long before we get it finished?'

'I'll put in some extra insurance policies to make sure you don't.'

Despite the playful tone in which she spoke these words they also came across as a thinly veiled threat.

Scene Five
Questionable Tactics

McGuire returned from his lunch with a newfound energy. His P.C equipment had arrived - complete with a printer. That had been a grave mistake on their part.

Giving McGuire his own printer in the workplace was as lethal as letting a blind school go on a field trip to a shooting range.

The I.T lads had informed him everything would be set up for him by the time he had returned from his dinner hour, and they had been true to their word.

Before going on his dinner break, McGuire had rifled through some of the stationary boxes to see if he could manufacture anything in order to help him with his mission a-la MacGyver style. In the end, he didn't need any elaborate contraptions to inspire him, just a good old-fashioned clipboard.

Soon after returning to his office, he had printed off various questionnaires to attach to his clipboard and set about introducing himself to the numerous employees of Play Dates that he had yet to meet. He had even printed off a pre-emptive certificate for his wall with this day's date on for his Hall of Shame. The category, Most amount of HR Complaints in a Single Day.

McGuire made his short pilgrimage to the office adjacent to his. The sign on the door read, Finance Department

He performed a polite knock and awaited the invite to enter. When it came, he was only too pleased to oblige.

'Good afternoon my new friends,' he greeted affably. 'My name's Barry McGuire and I'm from the Ideas and Development team. Jerry asked me to complete a questionnaire to ask our fellow employees in order to help us improve how we're perceived within the company.

'Good afternoon, Barry,' one of the middle-aged ladies

in the room spoke. Her name was Eileen. 'It's so nice to meet you.' McGuire couldn't help but notice that there was almost a condescending tone to the way she was speaking to him. It was although she thought he was a young child.

'Sure thing, we'd be delighted to answer your questions.'

He cleared his throat and proceeded to ask his question in a dry, nonchalant manner.

'Spit or Swallow?'

McGuire watched the rapid look of astonishment upon Eileen's face as she heard these words. Although this questionnaire was blurring the lines on whether it was a breach of Rule Number Six: Never Get Personal, he felt comfortable enough it wasn't a violation. Ultimately, it was a blanket series of questions with the goal of obtaining data, not any targeted insult.

To McGuire's surprise, she managed to suppress her outrage and was even able to give a polite smile before giving an answer. Her tone was somehow even more patronising than it had been before.

'I'm glad you're trying to make friends here Barry, but I don't think Jerry wrote that question and I don't think it's right that you should say he did. Nor is it right that you ask these questions. It's not your fault, and you're not in trouble. It was very nice to meet you.'

'Um, er, sure,' Barry replied flummoxed. 'Can I ask you the other questions on the questionnaire?'

'I tell you what, Barry. Why don't you leave them here with us and we'll hand them back to Jerry when we're done.'

'Transport me to the aquarium because there's something fishy going on,' Barry thought. He said nothing more though, instead he just handed the page of printed questions over to Eileen.

Even though she gave him a polite smile, he could see her eyes widen in astonishment as she browsed over some of the filth that had been written on the page.

And so, a similar pattern went as McGuire visited the

rest of the Play Dates offices and staff in the building. Even the H.R department appeared to walk on eggshells with how they spoke and addressed him.

He made his way perplexed and defeated as he trudged back to his office.

Victoria was standing outside the door with a smug smile on her face.

'Been busy Barry?' She asked, despite seemingly knowing the answer.

'What did you do?' There was no bitterness or resentment in his tone, just curiosity.

'Oh, just invoking that insurance policy I was telling you I had. After leaving your office after our little chat earlier, I sent an email to all the departments here, making sure to exclude yourself and Sebastian of course. I told them that as part of a new community outreach program we've got someone whose, what's the P.C way to say it - Mentally challenged - join us for a few weeks to live out his lifelong dream to be a part of the Play Dates family before his degenerative mental illness becomes too much for him.'

'Well played,' he spoke, genuinely impressed.

'I've got plenty more like that in the tank if I need it,' She replied with a broad smile. 'Just let me know when you want us to start working together Barry.'

Scene Six
Boxing Clever

Singer and Hensley were in their office, fretting over the declining sales numbers of some of Play Dates' legacy products. These were the same toys that had once brought the company to prosperity but were now deemed archaic and obsolete. Even a marketing campaign to rebrand them as "retro," didn't catch on with the consumers.

'Not good,' Singer spoke deflated.

'Not good at all,' Hensley concurred.

'If it's any consolation, at least our projections mean this company can stay afloat until after Sebastian passes. I don't think my heart could take it knowing he'd see this company fold before he does.'

'Shall I address the elephant in the room?' Hensley sighed.

'A McGuire shaped elephant?'

'McGuire, yes. That investment in his product can go a long way to this company keeping its head above water if it makes it to market and holds it own.'

'Do you really want to put all your faith and this company's success on the back of that imbecile?'

'I wouldn't even trust my kid's lunch money with that lunatic.'

'Besides' Singer added. 'Even if we were to rush that abomination of a product to market, we're still talking months away. I fear we need a miracle for this company to still be trading in even a year's time.'

Their morose conversation was interrupted by a voice calling for them from the other side of the door. The voice, they recognised. The accent – not so much.

It was McGuire, and he was speaking in what appeared to be a Medieval Olde English accent.

'Speak of the devil,' Hensley sighed.

'Come on ye out thou Southern heathens and faceth

thy retribution.'

'What on earth is that numpty up to now?' Singer spoke.

'Whatever it is, he's not busy working, that's for sure.'

Reluctantly, they opened their office door and stepped outside. They were immediately met with a scrunched-up paper ball being launched at them.

McGuire had blocked off the corridor outside their office with the boxes of paper from his office.

He had made a box fort and was stood behind it with a cardboard short sword cut out from one of the boxes.

'Hah hah hah foul infidels,' he mocked. 'I have cut off thou escape to yonder and thou are under siege. You heathens shall not lay terror across thy peasants lands any yore.'

He launched another paper ball at them.

'Barry!' Singer spoke in a raised and irate voice. 'Stop this madness at once and put all those boxes back to where you found them. This is a health and safety breach if ever I saw one.'

McGuire just smiled defiantly and tossed another paper ball at them.

'Oh, thank god.' Hensley spoke to Singer. 'It's Sebastian.'

McGuire, hearing these words, looked behind his shoulder and could see Undergrove walking his slow pace up the corridor. A look of confusion was already on his face.

'Your armies have outflanked me I see,' McGuire shouted to Singer and Hensley. 'But I will not go down quietly into this good night.'

McGuire threw some more paper balls, this time catching Singer on the forehead. Surely, with Undergrove as a witness a trip to HR would surely follow.

'What on earth is going on here?' Undergrove spoke when he finally made it to the box fort blocking the corridor.

'We're playing forts,' McGuire replied chipperly.

'No. We are not.' Singer asserted. 'Some of us are trying to work. Barry here is the one causing all the commotion.'

McGuire lobbed another paper ball at Singer. Technically this was not in violation of Rule 1. This was not physical violence, merely physical annoyance.

'Hush thy enemy's serpent tongue.'

'Are you going to stand for this Sebastian?

Undergrove contemplated for a moment, then a mischievous smile entered his face. He grabbed one of the sheets of paper from one of the opened boxes, scrunched it up and lobbed it at Singer. The throw may have been weak, but the intent was strong.

'You may take our lives, but you will not take our corridor,' he yelled.

The cough that followed may have weakened the impact of his declaration of revolt, but he was smiling, nonetheless. He encouraged McGuire to resume his attack - much to the astonishment of Singer and Hensley, who just stood there dumbfounded as to what they were witnessing.

Within minutes, a few more employees had come into the corridor to see what the commotion was about, and they too were bombarded by paper balls from the box fort. Unlike Singer and Hensley, however, they were only too eager to join in on the fun. They began to stock up on their own supplies of paper balls to return fire.

'Quick, Barry,' we need reinforcements, Undergrove ordered.

Barry began knocking the office doors on his side of the fort, and before long, a full-scale paper war had broken out in the corridor. McGuire noted the look of unadulterated joy on Undergrove's face.

'Look at them, Barry. They're all acting like big kids. I can't thank you enough.'

After the carnage of the paper fight had ended and the

employees had returned to their offices with a newfound spring in their step, Undergrove had a look in his eyes that McGuire hadn't seen before. Singer and Hensley who were still in the corridor recognised it though. It was a look they were only too thrilled to see. Undergrove's mind was working overtime.

'Harris, Giles,' he ordered with gusto. 'Call through to the Ideas and Development Team right now for an urgent meeting. We have a new product to develop.'

Scene Seven
Dead Cert

The hour was coming up to 21:00 and McGuire finally arrived back in Chelmsley Green via his coach.

It had been another unsuccessful day's playing his game and he was returning home still very much employed.

One person's failure, it would seem, is another's success, however.

Due to his antics in the office corridor, a brainstorming session between his team and Undergrove had seen another of McGuire's inadvertent ideas getting pencilled in for development. A soft play, build-your-own fort battle game, with easy storage and construction - and different themes for different battles as a separate accessory kit – for an additional cost of course. It had been delegated to Jaycon and Tina to work on with a view to getting it ready for an investment presentation within a month. Fun for the child, but just as much fun for the inner-child, Undergrove pitched it as.

He had given McGuire much of the credit though, and by the end of the meeting, McGuire couldn't help but feel he had been set up as some kind of saviour.

Even that dour duo of Singer and Hensley had given him a begrudging nod of approval by the end of the brainstorming session. McGuire's chances of dismissal now were looking very feint.

He made it to the front door of his home, tired, beleaguered, and for the moment, out of ideas.

Though his overwhelming desire was to slump himself down on the sofa, he knew he had something to check upstairs first.

Just as McGuire had expected, there was no stench of alcohol present in the spare room, just the surgical smell of disinfectant from where he had scrubbed the place clean earlier that morning.

'That klutz,' McGuire muttered, referring to his landlord. 'He's only gone and checked on the wrong bloody house.'

McGuire was about to leave the room and descend back downstairs to do his body and mind dirty by having a cheap and nasty microwave meal to accompany a no-thinking-required dumbass action movie - the more ridiculous the better. But then he saw it.

His eyes had only glanced over to his Hall of Shame for the briefest of moments, but that fleeting view was all he needed to sense that something about it was different.

There was a flash of red on one of the framed certificates.

McGuire went in closer to examine it and saw that the writing was written on the paper inside the glass frame.

The words were written in red crayon, quite possibly the same one he had used to apply for the Play Dates job. This deduction was made on account of him only possessing the one red crayon, and it not exactly being the kind of writing apparel intruders carried with them.

On the certificate for 'Fastest Firing,' part of the text had been obscured and written over with new words in the clumsy-looking red wax.

Stay away.

He surveyed some of the other certificates, and a justified sense of fear came over him when his eyes arrived at the location of the certificate for, Angriest Firing.

This one hadn't been doctored but had instead been replaced with a different certificate completely.

It had been typed out in identical font and formatting to its predecessor.

Days left before Death.

3

Scene Eight
Keeping Things P.C

Two police constables arrived approximately twenty minutes later.

McGuire relayed to them the smell of the animal urine, his landlord's conversation, and now the threats. There was no doubt in his mind that someone was playing games with him. Yet unlike the game he liked to play, this one was promising far more sinister outcomes.

'There's no sign of any forced entry,' the elder of the police constables spoke. He was aged in his early forties, balding, and his figure was beginning to display the signs of an unremovable middle-aged spread. He had introduced himself as Constable McVey. 'Do you know if anyone else has the key to your home?'

'No one aside from myself and my landlord as far as I know. I can give you his number if you like.'

'That would be grand if you could. We'll check with him to see if anyone has a spare, or if any previous tenants could still have access to your home.'

'Do you know of anyone who would have motive to threaten you this way, Mr McGuire?' The female constable inquired. She had introduced herself as PC Reeves. McGuire put her age in the early thirties, and though she was short, she looked physically fit and strong.

McGuire couldn't help but smile at her question.

'I've been known to make a few enemies in my time.'

'Yes,' McVey commented dryly. 'I've heard some of the stories about you. You're quite the local legend, Fire McGuire.'

Reeves threw her partner a look that suggested she wasn't privy to these stories and was intrigued to know more. McVey's wry smile and look he returned was one that indicated he would fill her in with more details later - now wasn't the appropriate time or place to do so.

'Do you think maybe this could be as a result of one of your firings?' his attention fell back to McGuire.

'It would make sense, I guess,' he conceded.

'Do you have a list of any of your former employers we can follow up on?'

'Sure thing. The paper copy I keep for my records was one of the documents that was destroyed this morning, but I have a hard copy on my PC. I can print you off another before you leave, no problem at all.'

'Thank you. Whoever it is has at least left us some form of evidence with their handwriting on one of your certificates. We may get lucky on our investigations and find a match to their style of lettering. Due to the severity of the threats, we'll do some dusting for prints too. It could be a shot to nothing, but sometimes it's those kind of shots that somehow land a bullseye. In the meantime, is there anywhere you can stay for a few nights, some family, or friends?' Reeves asked. 'If this is a personal vendetta, it may be better to go somewhere else for a while.'

McGuire pondered this question. The answer was that he hadn't anyone.

He had become estranged from his foster parents following Joseph's death, and as for friends, well, those who he could consider tight enough had all moved away and moved on with their lives. He had never really considered that he didn't have anyone close in his life anymore, his thoughts had always been too preoccupied with the game to contemplate any sense of loneliness.

'I'll be fine here for tonight,' he replied. 'Besides, if the note is to be believed, I won't be killed for another few days yet. I'll grab a B&B or hotel or something in London tomorrow and stay there until all this blows over. It will be easier for work anyway.'

'Ok, that sounds like a sensible idea. To be extra safe though we'll have a look at getting one of our constables to park up in their civilian car and keep an eye on the place just in case this person tries anything else in the meantime.'

'Thank you,' McGuire spoke with genuine gratitude.

'And if you can think of anything else that can help, I'll give you our number for the station and you'll come straight through to someone there directly instead of going through the switchboard.'

'Thank you again,' said McGuire.

After some more formalities, he shook their hands to say goodbye and to express his gratitude once more.

Scene Nine
Hammer Time

McGuire was alone in the house. His appetite had been replaced by the cocktail of fear, annoyance, and uncertainty, and it left a very unwelcome taste. His tiredness was still present, though this time he didn't want to submit to the fatigue. As much as he wanted to put his faith into the efficiency of the police constables, he had seen far too many thriller films where the wily antagonist had outfoxed the law enforcers under their very noses to catch their target unawares for a tense and bloody showdown. Granted, none of those films had been set in a village as small and as underwhelming as Chelmsley Green, but still, he was very much of the opinion that if you wanted someone you can really trust, then trust yourself. Even as he dwelled on this mantra, however, he did so with less assurance than he would have preferred.

If it was an ex-employer or former co-worker he had offended so much as a result of his game, enough to drive them to breaking and entering and death threats, then perhaps his life choices may not have been as frolicsome as he had perceived.

He took a seat in the spare room since this appeared to be the focus of the incidents so far. In his left hand, he held a mug of hot, triple-strength coffee, and in his right, he clasped tightly onto a claw hammer he'd found in one of the kitchen drawers, cluttered amongst various other dregs of DIY discards - a few Alan keys, a tape measure, and a perplexing assortment of screws which he had no idea how he had come to acquire.

If the intruder were to return this night, he would be waiting for them.

Part Six

Goodbye Chelmsley Green

Scene One
Shake Me Up Before You Go Go

The radio alarm clock sprang to life at 05:15. The offending tune was Wake Me Up Before You Go Go, by Wham.

Whoever this sick fuck of a DJ was for playing this annoyingly upbeat song at such a turd of an hour needed to be forced to listen to the aforementioned song, on loop, for the next 24 hours as punishment.

This overly chirpy song didn't exactly wake McGuire up before anyone went a go go since he was already partially awake - stuck in that muddled void between sleep and lucidness.

He observed that his claw hammer had been dropped onto the floor. He must have drifted off to sleep at some point and his grip softened when he succumbed to slumber.

It was only now that he realised what a foolhardy idea it had been in the first place. If the intruder had arrived when he'd drifted off and seen the hammer on the floor, he would have just handed him an additional choice of murder weapon.

McGuire performed a quick inspection of the house to ensure there had been no further incidents when he had been asleep. Satisfied that it was how he had last seen it and there were no new insidious traces, he proceeded to pack enough clothes into a holdall to last him about a week.

He didn't even shower before leaving his home for however long it would be. Again, he had seen far too many horror movies to allow himself to be exposed to some whacko in such a vulnerable position. Instead, he gave himself a Tramp Wash by dousing himself in Lynx Africa.

He had never considered himself to be a paranoid sort before, but maybe that was because previously he had never been given cause to. Even when he riled people through his antics, their anger at him had often been instantaneous. These threats were clearly premeditated. Yet, as he began his commute out of Chelmsley Green he was surveying everyone on the coach with suspicious eyes. His mind was working overtime trying to determine if there was anyone on this bus at this very early hour who had no reason to, other than to get a bit stalky.

Once he had made it to the connecting train and was sure no one was following him, he checked his bank balance via his mobile phone. He had just about enough funds in his account to cover him off for just under a week's lodging at a city hostel. Not ideal, by any stretch of the imagination. Yet again, he had seen far too many horror films to know that a stay in a strange hostel was never destined to end well.

He pondered to himself, given his current predicament, whether or not it would be best to put a pause on his playing the game for the immediate future and simply not turn up to Play Dates. After all, it was likely that it was his game that got him into this situation in the first place.

It didn't take long for McGuire to decide to continue playing. He studied statistics after all. When he broke it down in his mind, out of the dozens of employers he'd infuriated, and the hundreds of colleagues he'd offended, only one of them he'd upset enough to want to murder him - and when he weighed up the ratios, it really wasn't all that bad.

Scene Two
Taken to the Cleaners

The time was coming up to 09:45 and McGuire was sat at his desk hard at work. Hard at work in McGuire's world, however, didn't mean the same thing as most other employees' definition of the term. He was frantically jotting down on a notepad his previous firings and how they had occurred - along with the names of who had fired him. Maybe, retracing his abnormal memoirs may even give him a clue as to who the intruder to his home was. And, if nothing else, perhaps his notes would inspire some new techniques to get himself fired.

Despite the chaos he sowed with his antics, he was surprisingly organised when it came to documenting them - and was meticulously listing them in the jotter in alphabetical order.

He was working on the Cs on his index.

He had already finished writing down the accounts of his brief tenure working for a large cinema chain. He had been fired from that job in double quick time for trying to sell phone camera quality bootleg DVDs to the customers from behind the till of movies the cinema was showing.

Currently, he was finishing up the logging of his short time working as a cleaner for the cleaning company, Clean on Me.

A smile entered his face as he read back to himself the events that led to this dismissal. It had been a mere hour after he had started that he was approached by his supervisor, Katie Dart. She was flush in the face and slightly out of breath from her efforts in trying to find the newbie before he could cause any more damage.

'What the hell is wrong with you?' she asked as she approached him on the thirteenth floor.

'Well, one of my nipples is abnormally large, but that's a bit of a sensitive issue, quite literally.'

McGuire's attempt at humour was doing very little to soothe her obvious anger towards him.

'That's not what I mean, and you know it. I've been receiving numerous complaints from the managers up on the fifteenth floor you were assigned to cleaning. They were very distressed and weren't making much sense in what they were trying to say, so I went up and took a look for myself. There were chalk lines of bodies all over the hallway. It looked like some crime scene out of a detective show. They're freaking out up there that some kind of mass killing spree happened.'

'It was only meant as a practical joke.' McGuire attempted to explain. 'April Fool's Day is only seven months away, so I was trying to get them in the spirit and have a bit of fun.'

'They're chartered accountants on that floor, Barry. I don't think they appreciate fun. I think you better leave before there's a real chalk line of your body if I have to see you again.'

McGuire wrote the words, 'death threat spoken - possible suspect,' next to Katie Dart's name, though he did so without any real conviction.

He was about to write down the next occupation he had been fired from, which when placed in alphabetic order made it his cameo as a Croupier.

Just as the tip of his biro reconnected with the page of the notebook, he was interrupted by a knock at the door.

He recognised from the distinct sequence of knocks and the delicateness in which they were delivered as belonging to Victoria.

She didn't wait for a response, she just let herself in. She was holding a fold up computer chair and had strapped over her shoulder a laptop bag. She made her way silently and with purpose over to McGuire's desk.

McGuire watched dumbfounded as she unfolded the seat and set it up the opposite side of his desk and nonchalantly sat down facing him. She then opened the bag she had hanging by her side and pulled out her laptop and even more casually opened it up and started working on it. All the while, she did so without acknowledging him and acting as if this was the most natural thing in the world.

'Er, I think you have the wrong office,' McGuire spoke curtly.

'No, I have the right one,' she defied, finally speaking. 'Since you were dragging your heels yesterday about giving me an answer about working with you, I just thought I'd take the bull by the horns and make the decision on your behalf. Do strong independent women intimidate you, Mr McGuire?'

'Not at all. Feminist is one of my middle names you know.'

'Oh yeah,' Victoria humoured. 'And what are the others?'

'Charming Mother Fucker. The truth is you don't intimidate me one iota. I just don't like people getting too close in my personal space. I mean, this desk wasn't exactly designed for two.'

'Well, I think we can manage. Besides, my personal hygiene is above average, and lucky for you, I don't mind the smell of Lynx Africa. What the hell did you do, shower in that stuff?'

Victoria's eyes then noticed the holdall on the floor behind McGuire. 'Holy shit, you literally did, didn't you? What happened, did a besmirched girlfriend finally come to her senses and throw you out, or something?'

'Or something, yes.'

'Screw working. If I'm going to be all up in your personal space, I want to be all up in your personal life too. I'm intrigued. Wait, don't tell me what it is, I reckon I can guess it in three.'

'Oh, believe me,' McGuire defied. 'You definitely will need more than three guesses. Not unless you're some kind of psychopath.' McGuire allowed himself a long pause. 'In fact, I stand corrected. Maybe you would guess it in three.'

'Wow, your middle name really is Charming Mother Fucker isn't it. I tell you what. We'll make a game out of it. Do you like playing games?'

McGuire smiled.

'You could say that.'

'All right. Let's make it interesting then. If I can guess why you've been turfed out of your home within three guesses, then you agree to not only working with me, but you'll also take it seriously too - and with one hundred percent of your effort and commitment. No funny business.'

'And if you don't?'

'Then not only will I leave you in peace, but I will also even make a strong case to Sebastian to fire you.'

McGuire smiled a sincere smile at her.

'Pinky swear?' He asked.

'I'd even spit on you and shake your hand if you like.'

'Well, I'm not into that kinky shit, but let's just say we'll honour our words and mean it.'

'You're on,' Victoria challenged.

McGuire leaned back in his computer chair and placed his feet on the desk.

He was a picture of relaxation in an attempt to psyche out his nemesis and show her that he wasn't bothered by her impending guesses at all.

'Fire away,' he challenged, proceeded by a pantomime yawn of boredom.

'Okie dokey pig in a pokie,' she spoke confidently. She was showing no signs of being effected by any of his mind games. 'My first guess is that it's a maintenance issue. Judging by your dousing yourself in cheap deodorant it's likely a plumbing or water supply issue and you have no running water.'

'Wow check you out with your detective skills, Miss Marple.' McGuire spoke with thinly veiled sarcasm. 'Well, it looks like Nancy Drew just Nancy Drew a blank. You're one life down.'

Victoria let out a deep sigh.

'Ah well, not to worry. I'll get it with my next guess and wipe that smug smile off your face.'

She contemplated to herself for a while. Some of her musings she muttered aloud, others she kept to herself. 'Hmmm,' she muttered. 'You've already ruled it out being to do with your love life, and you've already indicated that it's not a conventional reason. Maybe, it's not to do with **your** home at all, maybe it's to do with a neighbour. Despite you coming across as a mess of a person, I wouldn't mind betting that secretly you're a bit of a control freak, and you moving out of your home for what looks like to be a few days, is to do with something out of your control and you can't handle that fact. Judging by the size of your holdall, you leaving seems short-term, so maybe it's to do with someone visiting. A child perhaps. Maybe they've just started learning a musical instrument and they're not exactly gifted in said instrument. You've already indicated your reason isn't a typical one, but maybe it's the instrument itself that isn't regular. It's got to be something loud and not something that would be someone's first choice of an instrument to learn. That would rule out violins, or recorders. I put it to you, Barry McGuire, you've moved out for a few days because your neighbour's child has been playing a Tuba - very badly and very incessantly.'

'Wow, I've never seen anyone be so wrong before for such a considered and elaborate answer. A part of me almost feels bad for the way you're embarrassing yourself in front of me right now.'

'Is that so?' Victoria spoke. 'Well, what would you say if I told you that I was just messing with you, and I already know the answer. It's because someone's been threatening your life and you're staying in London until it all blows over.'

McGuire's conceited expression was replaced by one

more aghast. It was now Victoria who displayed the superior look.

'Wha…how did you know?'

'You've left your notebook open Barry. I can see that you've written someone's name as a possible suspect because of a death threat they gave you.'

'Oh.'

'Seriously though Barry, what the hell! Are you ok?'

'Yeah, it's most likely nothing. But I guess it's better to be safe than murdered.'

'Where are you even staying? London's not cheap you know.'

'I still haven't looked. I was going to find somewhere in a little bit. Probably a hostel or something.'

'No chance. Look, you're my meal ticket in getting my ideas to market and I've got to make sure you're looked after. I know Jayce is looking for a house mate, and I know he'd be more than happy to put you up for a week or so for free of charge. He'd be glad of the company.'

'That's very kind, and no offence to Jaycon, but I'd rather go back to my own home and get skinned alive by some murderous psychopath. Even if I found his personality less sufferable, it would be the worst possible variant of the Fallow Formula.'

'What the hell are you talking about?'

'Long story, but basically it means living with someone you work with means even less time away from having to deal with your job as no doubt the majority of conversations would be work related.'

Victoria let out a sigh.

'I'm going to regret this, but I have a spare room too. And I categorically promise you that I will not talk shop with you. Quite frankly, I doubt I'll even want to talk to you at all. And it will only be for a few days, right.'

'Why are you doing this?'

'I told you, it's for purely selfish reasons. I'm looking out for my Trojan Horse, well, technically, it's a Trojan

Vibrator.'

'I don't think it's for selfish reasons at all. Quite the opposite in fact.'

'It's as I said, I'm actually a nice person deep down when you get to know me. And despite your extreme efforts, I think that maybe you are too. In any case, we had a bet, and one that I won. We're a team now.'

Scene Three
Urine Too Deep

Much of the morning's "work," with Victoria had consisted of them drawing up terms to their working and living agreement.

It was during these negotiations that one of the cardinal rules of McGuire's games had been broken. Rule Eight: Never tell anyone of your game – ever.

Technically, it wasn't McGuire who was at fault for this violation, and therefore, after a self-performed steward's enquiry, no disqualification from the game was deemed necessary. The fault of the breaking of this rule fell solely on Victoria - All McGuire really did was save time by filling in the blanks for her – and he only did this since she would have eventually figured out those parts for herself too.

She had already worked out from the behaviour of his first two days that he was trying to get fired. She had already told him as much previously. What she didn't know back then was to why. But, despite her earlier declaration that she didn't care what his reasons were, now that he had agreed to work with her on his project, she quickly found that she did care very much indeed. And she knew that if McGuire wouldn't talk, then perhaps his notebook would.

'They still haven't cleaned that window from where that poor bird flew into it,' she'd observed with a nonchalant interest looking up from her laptop.

Without thinking, McGuire's gaze instinctively veered towards the window.

'Sucker,' Victoria mocked as she swiped his previously guarded notebook and made a dash towards the doorway so she could at least skim the contents for some titbits before McGuire got up to try and retrieve it.

Gone for now was her frosty exterior and burden of

guilt over Niles. She was feeling and acting like a child again - and it felt good.

Even though McGuire had only gotten as far as documenting up to the letter C in his journal, there was still enough damning evidence for Victoria to work out that this was all part of a game to him.

'Well, it's more interesting than playing tiddlywinks,' she sighed.

With the cat now out of the bag, McGuire saw no harm in revealing his motives for playing it. He told her of Joey and his suicide – something she understood only too well having seen Niles' demise. He then told her of the Fallow Formula, and though she was more sceptical of this motive, McGuire did at least make sense in some of the things he was saying - and his passion in explaining it was admirable, if nothing else.

What came across the most, however, as McGuire regaled his reasons for playing the game - for better or worse, was just how much he enjoyed it, and for that alone Victoria couldn't judge him too much.

As part of their terms of them working together they agreed that Victoria wouldn't tell anyone else of his game, and she would even allow him to continue to play it - provided he didn't pull any of his shit with her or the product they would be working on.

They had also agreed that if they were to be sharing an office together, then space would be key. All the stationary, and boxes would need to be removed to allow room for a second desk. As such, McGuire had taken an early and extended lunch to allow the maintenance guys time to get the new desk set up.

Upon returning to his office, the sight McGuire came back to was not one that he had anticipated. The stacks of boxes had been removed and the new desk set up as arranged. Yet stood in the corner of the room was a figure with his back to McGuire urinating against the wall.

'Hey!' McGuire yelled with justifiable astonishment.

'What the hell do you think you're doing?'

The figure slowly turned around. McGuire recognised him immediately. He had seen him once before - on his first day here. He was even wearing the same sand-coloured suit. The stranger said nothing. He just stared at McGuire through his dishevelled eyes for an awkward amount of time before leaving the room.

There weren't many moments in his life that McGuire could claim to be truly dumbfounded by someone's actions. Usually, the roles would be reversed. Yet the audaciousness over what had just happened left him perplexed.

He made his way over to his holdall and pulled out his trusty can of deodorant. It wasn't exactly Febreze, but it would make an adequate substitute. The smell of urine was a potent one. Whoever this whacko was, he definitely needed more hydration in his diet. As he began to spray in the offending corner, he decreed that there was no point in calling Maintenance, since it was one of their team who had decided to piss all over the place in the first instance. Nor would he tell anyone about it. He didn't think he could stand the thought that someone got fired before he could. If it wasn't for Rule Three – No Destruction of Property - he may even have followed suit.

Not that getting fired in such a cheap way was something McGuire favoured, he had a far more outrageous plan in mind; and with Victoria yet to return from her break, now was the perfect opportunity to set it in motion.

Though some would say it would be counterproductive for him to spend much of the money that he had saved by taking up Victoria's offer of a place to stay for a few days, he saw it as an investment opportunity. That investment was in an irresistible firing opportunity.

Scene Four
Strip Searched

The time was coming up to 15:00 and some good progress had been made between Victoria and McGuire in finding ways to incorporate her product into his without jeopardising the look of it too much. Ultimately, it still looked like a vibrator with a face, but at least it was a vibrator with a face that would help develop social skills.

Their collective focus on the task was suddenly interrupted by the sound of McGuire's digital Casio watch alarm sounding off.

'I've got to shoot,' he said as he got up from his chair with haste.

'What? Go where?

'I've got a stripper to meet out the front,' his nonplussed reply came as if it was the most natural answer that could have come.

******

McGuire made his way out to the front of the Play Dates building, where a woman aged in her early twenties and dressed in the sluttiest nurse attire conceivable was waiting patiently for him. Judging by her wild and dilated eyes, it was more than a little Dutch courage present in her bloodstream.

He had found this stripper's number via a Google search and had come across (not literally) an erotic dancer version of Trip Advisor – the aptly named Strip Advisor.

Having determined the cheapest rated club on the site, he had given the venue a call to ask if any of their performers were available for "corporate events."

'Candy?' McGuire asked needlessly as he approached the stripper. Unless it was the worlds least appropriately dressed nurse, and the NHS was trying some radical new scheme, there was no doubting who this person was.

'I'm Candy Cane,' the stripper confirmed. 'Though just to let you in on a little secret, that's not my real name.' She was being sincere when she spoke this last part. McGuire couldn't help but wonder just what level of customer's intelligence she was used to.

'Well, Miss Cane, are you ready to put on a show?'

Stripadvisor®

****

'Hi Kimmy,' McGuire spoke as he approached the reception desk. Candy was close behind him, already drawing aghast looks from those loitering around the foyer.

'Hi Barry,' she spoke. 'How's your day going?'

'All is well, my fair lady,' he spoke jovially, borderline flirtingly.

Kimmy blushed slightly before her gleaming face turned into one of confusion and awkwardness as her attention turned to the inappropriately dressed female standing behind McGuire. He was quick to spot her reaction.

'This is Nurse Cane,' he sought to clarify. 'She's here to

give the Ideas and Design Team their medicals. It's a new initiative Sebastian is trialling.'

Kimmy remained unconvinced.

'Why's she dressed like that?'

'For medical reasons, I can't elaborate on,' his instant reply came.

Kimmy was having none of it.

'Then what about the leather whip she's carrying?'

'It's to test their reflexes. Due to health and safety legislation it's been deemed safer than a reflex hammer.'

'I'm sorry, Barry, but I don't believe you're telling the truth. I can't let her have a clearance pass.'

McGuire let out an apologetic smile.

'I understand, Kimmy,' he spoke dejectedly. 'But can I just say one more thing?'

'Of course, Barry.'

'Run!'

McGuire grabbed the stripper by the hand and sprinted towards the elevator.

'Stop!' Kimmy shouted after them, but it was no good. They had already made it into the lift.

****

'Thank god I didn't go for the donkey package,' McGuire wheezed as they made it inside the elevator and he had pressed the up button.

The Play Dates jingle began playing and he was quick to notice Candy's face turn from flush to one of sadness. Tears were starting to form in her eyes.

'Hey, are you okay?' he asked.

'It's this song,' she replied.

'Yeah, I get you sister. It drives me mad too.'

'I remember this tune from my childhood. I used to love the Play Date toys as a kid, and I'd badger my father no end to buy me whatever product was being advertised on the television. I would sing this song to him over and

over and over until he'd cave in and buy me one.'
Her tears were falling harder now.
'He was a good man, I can't tell you how much I miss him.'
'Hey now,' McGuire tried to calm. 'Dry those tiny tears now. No one enjoys a lap dance off someone crying.'
'Actually, I've had some customers pay extra for that,' the reply came – rather awkwardly for McGuire, she didn't seem to be saying it in jest.
'Wow, this has taken a turn,' he rued aloud.

****

McGuire didn't wait to be summoned upon knocking enthusiastically upon his old office's door. He just let himself in.
From the looks that were sent his way from Jerry, absence most definitely didn't make the heart grow fonder, it just served as a reminder of how much more tranquil it had been in the meantime.
'Hey guys,' McGuire spoke.
The greeting was returned with varying degrees of enthusiasm. Jaycon's response seemed amiable enough. He couldn't determine Tina's as it was so muted, and Jerry's was as abrupt as he had become accustomed to. It was exactly how he wanted it to be.
'Hey Jerry,' he spoke with his mock sincerity. 'Why are you such a grumpy bunny with me today. I bet you I can turn that frown upside down.'
Jerry's scowl remained unmoved by this wager. Any promise from McGuire about turning that "frown upside down," not only implied it would result in the opposite, but make his stomach curdle with apprehension too.
'I haven't got time for this, Barry.'
'But I've brought you a very special gift.'
Jerry let out a pre-emptive sigh. It proved to be well justified as McGuire began to play the tune, 'If you think

I'm sexy,' by Rod Stewart via his mobile phone.

'If this is what I think it is,' he snapped. 'Then you better think again, or you'll be out of a job.' The threat came, much to McGuire's secret delight.

The volume of the song was turned up and McGuire beckoned for Candy to do her stuff.

As she came into view, however, Jerry's irked expression turned into one of amazement. He hadn't even seemingly acknowledged the sluttish attire she was wearing. He was only focussed on her face.

'Cynthia?'

Candy's wild eyes suddenly became more focussed as she stared at the middle-aged man sat behind the desk. There was to be no performing of her act. She had remained frozen in place through shock. Despite the years that had passed since she had last seen this face, there was no mistaking the blemishes upon it.

'Dad, is that you?'

Tears began to flow down Jerry's face, yet McGuire could sense these were happy tears - and if this stripper was indeed his daughter, they were not a reaction one would expect a father to have at seeing his daughter turn up to his workplace in a slutty nurse outfit.

Jerry bounded from his desk and embraced Candy, or as he had now revealed her real name to be, Cynthia.'

'I thought I'd lost you forever,' he sobbed uncontrollably. 'I even took a job at Play Dates as a way to still be close to you somehow. I know how much you loved these toys as a kid, and I held onto some crazy notion that you would see one advertised on the television, or in a shop one day, and know that it was me who designed it as a way of saying I love you.'

'I'm so sorry I ran away,' Cynthia's tearful reply came. 'I was too ashamed over who I've become and the life choices I've been making ever since to contact you. I thought you'd hate me for who I'd become.'

'None of that matters now, all that matters is that we

found each other again.'

The embrace was even tighter now, it was as if they never wanted to let each other go.

A bemused McGuire turned the song off from his phone. It wasn't really fitting with the mood he'd intended anyway.

'How did you know I was here?' Jerry spoke amazed.

'I didn't!' Cynthia replied. 'It was that guy over there.' She pointed over to McGuire. 'He contacted me and said there was someone special he wanted me to meet. He said this person had been down in the dumps these past few days and wanted to do something special for him.'

'Is this true, Barry?' Jerry enquired, drying his eyes with his tie.

'Er, kind of.' His uncertain reply came.

Technically, he had told this stripper that there was someone he'd like her to perform for and for a few extra quid to make the striptease extra special. He guessed that the mixture of whatever substances were still in her body, along with the overwhelming emotion of the remarkable reunion had skewed the authenticity of what had been said.

In any case, McGuire felt the warm and tight embrace from Jerry now. The happy tears were flowing again.

'I am forever indebted to you,' he gushed. 'When Cynthia ran away from home when she was sixteen years old, her mother and I feared we'd never find her again, and with each passing day, those fears were increasingly becoming a reality. But you've brought her back home to us.'

Tina came up to join the others, she was carrying her long, thick coat, and handed it over to Cynthia to cover herself up. She then threw McGuire a smile of acknowledgement that suggested perhaps he wasn't the devil she'd originally believed him to be.

Although he couldn't deny the happiness he felt over Jerry being reconciled with his daughter, a part of him still couldn't help but rue his rotten luck. Whilst the stars had somehow aligned for his manager, they had dispersed all together from him.

Scene Five
Making a Meal Out of Things

McGuire couldn't help but notice Victoria smiling at him from her desk.

'Have I got something on my face?' he asked with sincerity as he made an instinctive wipe against his mouth with his sleeve.

'I would say only egg on it,' she quipped. 'But I don't believe that to be the case at all. You've come out of this looking like a hero yet again. I don't know how the hell you do it.' There was a long pause before she spoke again. 'Do you believe in destiny, Barry?'

He shook his head to say no.

'I never used to either,' she said. 'I'm very much a black and white, everything has an explanation if you look hard enough, kinda person. Luck isn't really luck at all. It's just a thing that statistically happens from time to time, and our lives are just so humdrum that when that spike in good fortune does happen, it just seems more remarkable than what it really is. But what you pulled today, isn't even a million to one shot, it far surpasses that.'

'Nah, not at all. I studied statistics in uni, and it's much lower than you think. Look at it, if you had Jerry as a father, the odds are probably one in four that you'd develop a drink or drugs problem and want to run away from home.'

'Don't be so mean, Barry. The more I get to know you, the more it doesn't seem a natural fit.'

'Whatever. Ok, let's call the odds one in ten that she'd want to run away. Is that being nicer?'

Victoria scoffed.

'Anyway, **statistically,** the career prospects of a runaway female, as harsh as it sounds, is likely to end up with something in the sex industry.'

'Even if that's true,' Victoria countered. 'What would

be the odds, **statistically,** of you playing your game and being debauched enough to actually hire a stripper for your manager who turns out to be her father?'

McGuire said nothing to this, much to Victoria's smug delight.

'Like it, or not, Barry, I think you're supposed to be here. It's your destiny - and I've seen enough cheesy films in my life to know that you can't fight destiny. It has a way of catching up with you sooner or later. Why else do you think that every shitty thing you've done here turns into gold?'

It was McGuire's turn to scoff now.

He was grateful for his defeat in this debate being interrupted by a knock on the door followed by a cough.

'Come in, Sebastian,' Victoria shouted.

The door opened and Undergrove's frail figure filled the space to the best of its faultering ability. Despite the sad figure his body projected, his beaming smile still shone bright upon it.

'There they are. My dream team. My dynamic duo. I just thought I'd swing by personally and pass on my own gratitude to you Barry, for what you did for Jerry.'

Victoria threw McGuire another sly smile.

'We're all family here, and you've really embraced that ethos with what you did for Jerry, despite your differences. That goes a long way in my book. Which brings me onto you Victoria. I have great news for you too. Jerry has requested an indefinite leave of absence so he can catch up on lost time with his daughter and to focus on getting her the help she needs to get herself back on track. Lost time may be something that can never truly be found again, but only a mean-hearted soul would deny them the time they have ahead to make up for it. It was the least I could do for them. This of course leaves a management position open in the team, and I can't think of anyone more suited or worthy than yourself.'

'Thank you,' she spoke, unable to hide the beaming

smile on her face.

'The thanks are all mine. As such, I would like to take you both to dinner this evening. Nothing too fancy, but still fancy enough to show my gratitude.'

He couldn't help but see the displeasure on McGuire's face.

'Don't make me play the "old dying man" guilt card on you Barry. I'm not above playing it, you know. This dinner together will be purely for pleasure, no talking shop at all, I promise. I would love to get to know you both better before I get to no longer know you at all.'

Begrudgingly, Barry had no choice but to indulge Undergrove.

'No work talk, right?' he confirmed.

'I swear.'

'Okay, but if you break that promise, I get to punch you in the dick, deal.'

Undergrove laughed and bid his farewell.

Scene Six
The Waiting Game

The Wishing Tree restaurant was only a short walk from Victoria's home, and Undergrove had chosen it for that reason, despite it being more of a hardship for him to get to. Yet he had insisted upon it.

McGuire looked distinctly underdressed as he escorted Victoria into the Wishing Tree restaurant. She looked beautiful in her sleek crimson dress which only enhanced his incongruous attire of his faded blue denim jeans and unbranded white t-shirt. Victoria had offered him some shirts and a tie that she still had stored in her home, but upon learning that they had belonged to Niles, McGuire politely declined.

'I'm not stepping out in a dead man's suit,' he thought, yet didn't comment aloud, out of fear of upsetting Victoria. It was probably best that he didn't take her up on the offer of the hand me downs anyway, he didn't want to dredge up any suppressed feelings over her late boyfriend.

A part of him even hoped they would turn him away from this fine establishment for not meeting their dress code. Yet, despite some dirty looks from the Maitre De and a number of the diners, he was let in without too much protest.

The time was coming up to 20:00.

McGuire and Victoria had been sat at their table for quarter of an hour and had already been deep into their first bottle of wine, whilst making the most of the no work talk edict and conversing over favourite films, music, and books.

Though she was loathe to admit it of her companion, he clearly wasn't the buffoon she'd originally had him pegged down as. He was clearly well-educated - and despite his juvenile antics, he had refined tastes when it came to culture. Knowing this made her angry at him too, though she daren't ruin the pleasant evening thus far by berating him. This oddity of a man had so much potential to offer the world, yet he opted to squander it partaking in that ridiculous game of his.

With the strict mandate of no work talk between them in enforcement, Victoria and McGuire needed to get creative in their conversations. Partially influenced by the bottle of wine they were consuming rather too quickly between them, soaked up only by a couple of complimentary bread rolls as they awaited Sebastian's belated arrival before ordering their meal, their dialogue quickly steered towards the absurd. Topics over questions such as, whether the True Love from the song 12 Days of Christmas was just being overzealous with the lavishness of her daily gifts, or whether she was, in all reality, merely bat shit crazy with more red flags than a communist march.

Questions over whether Wile E. Coyote in the Roadrunner cartoons was the true hero of the show, and his pursuit of the Roadrunner was a deep-rooted metaphor for pursuing the promise of a happiness they will always get close to but never succeed in getting hold of.

In their defence, it was a pretty strong wine.

The flow of the conversation was halted by Victoria taking a glance over at her watch.

'Sebastian's running late, I hope everything's okay.'

'I wouldn't be so sure,' McGuire spoke wryly. 'This is the moment where he reveals himself to be an evil genius all this time. He's going to stand us up and leave us drunk and with a massive booze bill just for shits and giggles.'

Victoria smiled.

'Sebastian hasn't a cruel bone in his body. He's a rare kind of person these days sadly. The world will be a worse place for losing him but a better place for knowing him.'

McGuire returned the smile. Their gazes locked with each other for a prolonged moment. Victoria blushed slightly and turned her head towards the waiter.

'Tell me, Barry. Have you ever been fired from being a waiter. You only got as far as the C words in your journal, and I don't mean the four-letter variety.'

'I have indeed. Believe it or not, that was one of the more challenging jobs to get fired from.'

'Really? I would have thought it easy as pie. Surely all you'd have to do is keep getting orders wrong or dropping the platefuls of food all the time.'

'That would be a violation of the rules, never cause damage to property, and never do anything that could lose business or their reputation. The key to playing the game is making the firing and any outrage all about yourself, not the business. I may be an asshole ma'am but I aint no monster.

'I'm starting to think that maybe you're not the asshole you think you are. Troublesome, yes. Antagonistic, for sure. Unhinged, undeniably. But I think you do have a sweet side to you that's just bursting to be let out.'

'Wow, that drink really has gone to your head if you think that.'

'So how did you do it? Get fired from being a waiter I mean.'

A smile came to McGuire's face as he recalled the events and began to narrate them to Victoria

The restaurant in question had been Valentinos, an Italian restaurant a few miles away from Chelmsley Green. This had been in the fledgling stages of McGuire playing his game, and as such, his reprehensible reputation had yet to be known to the locals and its surrounding areas.

The proprietor and manager of Valentinos was a gentleman named Harry Pike, far less an authentic Italian name than the food the restaurant was serving.

It had taken an hour into McGuire's first shift for him to be summoned into Pike's office.

'You called for me boss?' he spoke.

'Yes, I called for you, Barry. What the hell is going on here? It's come to my attention that you're trying to take over this restaurant from the inside and claim it as your own.'

'What on earth gives you that ridiculous idea?' McGuire replied.

'Because I've had some of the kitchen staff come up to me informing me that you approached them telling them you were going to take over this restaurant from the inside and claim it as your own, and that you would match their wages if they helped you.'

'It's just their word against mine,' McGuire scoffed. 'That doesn't prove a thing.'

Pike was having none of it and held aloft Exhibit A. It was a handful of the restaurant menus. Upon them, the name Valentinos had been scribbled out in blue biro and Barry's Bistro had been written above the scribbles.

'I've been framed,' he spoke, purposely unconvincingly.

'Then how do you explain then the reports from some of the customers I've been speaking to, saying that you've been welcoming them to, "Barry's Bistro," and that you only accept PayPal payments under your name?'

'It's a conspiracy.'

'It's outrageous is what it is. It's not so much a military coup but a culinary one. I've never seen anything so audacious in all my time as a restauranteur. You're fired.'

Victoria looked astonished upon hearing this story.

'I'm starting to think that maybe you're a sociopath, Barry. Tell me, is it worth it? Going through all these efforts and plans to play this game of yours? I mean its nuts, right.'

'Any more nuts than those jumping out of an aeroplane for fun, or climbing Everest just to say they've done it?'

'I guess not.'

Their conversation was interrupted by a waiter coming to their table carrying a mobile phone.

'I'm sorry to interrupt you both, but I have a Sebastian Undergrove on the phone, and he would like to speak to you both.'

The waiter handed the phone over to Victoria.

'Sebastian, it's Vic, is everything okay?' there was a short pause whilst Victoria listened attentively before a coughing fit came from the other end of the line, forcing her to hold the phone as far from her ear as her arm span permitted. Even from the opposite side of the table, McGuire could hear the splutters. Once the coughs had subsided, Victoria spoke to him again.

'Of course, Sebastian, I'll bring him over now.'

She gestured with her free hand for McGuire to come over to her. 'He wants to speak to us both.'

McGuire squatted next to her chair and leant into the phone in her hand, both Victoria and he became aware they were practically cheek to cheek.

'Hey, Sebastian,' McGuire spoke to make him aware he was on the line now. 'You're not ditching us with the bill now, are you?'

'Yes and no,' his reply came. 'Don't worry about the bill, it's as I said earlier, its my little way of saying thank you to you both. I've given the staff there the strictest instructions to encourage you both to get irresponsibly drunk and to put it all on my card. You two have helped this company in ways I don't think you fully appreciate yet, so it's only right that you get to let loose. As for ditching you. Well, yes that part of it, I am.

Truth be told, I never intended to show up in the first place. This is your night and your night alone. You don't want to have it spent with an uncool old man like me cramping up your style and fun. Heck, I'm not even in London right now.

An opportunity has arisen for some experimental treatment for my illness, and I am on my way to undergo proceedings. It's the last roll of the dice if you will - and when you've got nothing to lose, then it's not really that much of a gamble, more of a hail mary.

I'll be gone for a week or so, maybe longer. Who knows.

In any case, enjoy the night and don't scrimp on the drink. Thank you again. For everything.'

The phone call ended.

Neither Victoria nor McGuire dared say it out loud, but they knew what that phone call was. 'Thank you again, for everything,' was Undergrove's way of saying farewell to them forever.

Scene Seven
Picture This

That night, McGuire's sleep was an unsettled one.
If to not scrimp on the wine was Undergrove's decree, then who was he to deny a man their dying wish?
He'd staggered into the spare room with the all the dexterity and grace of a pantomime villain in an old cowboy film, who had been wounded by the heroic gunslinger.
The drunken words he had expressed to Victoria in gratitude for a good night's company weren't reciprocated so sweetly. She was too busy hunched over the toilet basin ejecting much of the wine she had consumed.
McGuire belly flopped onto his bed.
He closed his eyes to the world to help combat the spinning of the room.
He was unsure how long he had been asleep for, if it could even be classed as sleep at all - but unconsciousness caused by the excess alcohol. What was for certain, however, was the image he had seen that brought him back to cognizance.
The speed in which he bolted upright caused a sudden pain to his head, yet the intense throbbing was overwhelmed by the nauseous churning in his stomach - only these feelings were caused by distress, not the toxins still present in his bloodstream.
The vision he had seen had been that of his brother, Joseph - or at least it had resembled him to begin with.
He was standing at the foot of the bed of the spare room McGuire was currently staying in.
His lips were moving upon his distressed face as if he was warning him about something. Yet, no sound vacated his mouth. Get out, were the words he appeared to be mouthing. Then his flesh began to rapidly rot. He was

scratching at it as if to soothe the itch yet was only succeeding in scraping the rancid skin away from bone, leaving a monstrous image of shredded flesh and tissue.

McGuire struggled for breath as he exited the bed and got to his feet.

His legs were unsteady, but he doubted that was to do with the alcohol still in his system. Then the smell hit him, it was the smell of something rotten in the room. He sprinted for the bedroom window and opened it. He would never describe London air as fresh air, yet as the cold and the breeze of the outside hit him, it was enough to allow him to breathe easier and suppress that disoriented feeling.

Once he had calmed himself, he made a check on his Casio watch for the time. It was a little past 03:00.

With the nightmarish image still fresh in his mind, he knew that trying to get back to sleep was an exercise in futility. It would appear that his day had begun early.

With his skin clammy and his mind still groggy, a shower would be what the doctor ordered. Well, technically, the doctor would have ordered that he only drink in moderation and not the excess volume he had consumed last night.

Following the shower and feeling close to human again, he made his way over to the kitchen to make a cuppa. It may not be a miracle cure for a hangover, or vivid nightmares, but it sure as shit would comfort him a little.

He took his brew to the breakfast bar and was quick to notice laying on there was a framed photograph. He was certain it hadn't been there upon his last visit to this table yesterday evening - before leaving for the restaurant. He figured Victoria must have put it there at some point after her hot date with the toilet bowl.

He recognised the couple in the photograph immediately, Victoria being one of them, the other that weirdo from the maintence department he had caught urinating in his office.

They were the picture of happiness in the photograph, standing in front of Nelson's Column. Both were smiling, and that nutjob, even wearing that same sandy suit, had his arm embraced around her. Things started to make more sense to him now. That asshole wasn't pissing against the office wall to make some statement against him, he was doing it against Victoria. Probably as revenge for realising she was too good for him.

He reasoned that she must have retrieved the photograph due to her feeling sorry for herself for whatever reason, and like a plethora of others before her, perhaps she had been contemplating making a reckless or bad decision at the behest of too much alcohol.

In any instance, it was none of his business — wasn't it?

Part Seven

Game Over

Scene One
Low Maintenance

Upon dwelling on it for the morning and allowing time enough for the worst of Victoria's and his hangovers to mercifuly ebb away, he'd decided to tell her of what her ex-boyfriend, the maintenance man, had done in their office.

The swaying factor for him coming forward was that she had become something McGuire couldn't say he had many of in his life, a friend, and as such, he respected her enough to tell her the events so that she could make her own decision on how she would like to handle it.

'So, that ex of yours is a bit of an asshole, I'd watch out for him,' he said once one of their brainstorming sessions on trojan horsing the Krazy Cucumber had come to a natural conclusion.

Victoria was taken aback.

'Well, first of all. With my dating history that narrows down who you're talking about to a couple of dozen. Secondly, what right do you have to make comments about my personal life?'

'Isn't that what friends do?' he said with uncharacteristic sheepishness.

Victoria smiled.

'Yes, I guess it is. So, tell me Bazza, me old chum, which one of my delightful exes is the asshole in question, and how do you know about them?'

'It's that maintenance worker. I caught him pissing in the corner of our office the other day.'

'Ewwww, you caught someone pissing in our office and you didn't say anything? And if it's any small consolation, at least I'm exonerated in the asshole-ex stakes for this one. I've never dated anyone from maintenance.'

'Well, he was the same guy who was in that photograph you left in the kitchen after our night out. You know, the one with the sand-coloured suit in front of Nelson's Column.'

Victoria turned ashen as she heard these words. She looked at McGuire in the eyes intently for a prolonged moment, then left without saying a word.

For the remainder of the day, it was clear that she was avoiding him under the transparent guise of using her duties covering Jerry's role as an excuse. The vibrant, full of vigour person he had come to know this past few days had been replaced by a distant stranger. Even when they had left the office and were back in her flat, she had made it her clear intention to avoid him.

The following morning followed the same pattern with her avoidance and was showing no sign of abating.

McGuire had been alone in his office, busy writing in his journal.

He wasn't documenting his previous firings as had once been the jotter's purpose. Instead, he was on his fifth or sixth draft of an apology letter to Victoria for getting involved in her personal life. The way he saw it, giving the perfect apology was like walking a tightrope without a safety net. Get it wrong and the results would be even more devastating.

He was interrupted mid-sentence by the sound of ringing on his mobile phone. The caller number was showing as unknown.

'Barry McGuire speaking,' he answered.

'Barry, its PC McVey,' the rattled voice came. 'Is now a good time to talk?'

'It depends, I guess. Theres always a perfect time to hear the good news, but never the right time to hear the bad. What's the update?'

McGuire had already determined by McVey's tone during his introduction that this was likely to be the latter.

'It appears we've hit a dead lead,' the hesitant reply came.

'Ah, ok. Well, thank you for the update,' McGuire

replied. 'The wholly unnecessary update,' he continued in his mind.

'No, what I mean to say is the suspect we have is literally dead. The follow up checks PC Reeves and myself did with the fingerprint checks on your certificate frame returned a positive match on our national criminal database.

About a month ago a gentleman got arrested for being drunk and disorderly in the Southwest area of London. Long story short, he caused destruction to some public property and resisted arrest. No charges were filed against him, and he was let off with a caution. Anyway, his prints matched up to those we found in several locations of your home. As did some of the lettering on the signature on his release form to that on the threat which was written on your certificate. Does the name Niles Malone mean anything to you?'

A shiver came over him.

'He used to be an employee at the company I started at this week, Play Dates. He killed himself a few months ago. It's his old team I'm currently working in.'

'Well, I guess that establishes a connection between you both, but it doesn't help make any more sense out of it. I've got to tell you, McGuire, it's got me really stumped as to how those fingerprints ended up all around your home. Obviously, there's got to be some kind of explanation, and for my own sanity, I'm going to figure out what it is. In any case, I thought I'd just give you a call to let you know. If you need me at all or have any ideas as to what the hell is going on, don't hesitate to call, okay.'

The phone call ended.

McGuire made a quick exit from his office. He had to find Victoria.

Scene Two
That's the Spirit

McGuire burst into his old office without even a precursory knock.

'Hey, Bazza,' Jayce beamed upon seeing his dramatic entrance. 'Whassup?'

'Fuck you Jayce and start wearing t-shirts of bands you've actually listened to.'

'Dude!' Jayce responded aghast.

'Barry!' Victoria scolded. 'That's no way to speak to your colleagues.'

'Then either fire me or talk to me. That guy I saw in my office, wasn't a maintenance guy, was he?'

Victoria looked skittish, frightened even.

'We'll talk over coffee somewhere. There's no way I'm going back in your office, and there's no way I'm discussing it here.'

****

McGuire noticed the tray carrying the two coffees shaking in Victoria's hands as she brought the drinks over to the table they had procured at a nearby cafe.

'What the hell is going on?' McGuire cut straight to the chase. 'I've just had the police phone me saying that I've got the fingerprints of your dead boyfriend all over my house. And since I told you about seeing some guy pissing in our office who was also in a photo with you, you haven't stepped foot anywhere near there. It was Niles I saw, wasn't it?'

Victoria nodded her head solemnly.

'Is he alive? I mean, he could have faked his death, right? I'm no expert but jumping in front of the train won't leave much of a body. Maybe it was a case of identifying the wrong person as the deceased. The police said there had to be a logical reason, and it's as I often say, sometimes in life the correct answers to the most challenging questions are often the easiest.'

'No. He's definitely dead,' she sighed. 'They identified him by the CCTV footage at the train station. He was even wearing that same sand-coloured suit you saw him in. Ever the considerate person, he even placed his wallet on the platform floor before he jumped, to help the authorities identify him. What a giver, right?

At first when you told me about what happened in your office, I considered that it was another one of your pranks, or schemes to get fired. Shit, I even hoped it was. There were a few things that convinced me you were telling the truth though.

First of all, that urinating incident in this office happened when he was still working here. I went in there once to check in on him and found him relieving himself. It was when his drinking was getting worse than ever. I never told a soul about it and covered it up. That was the last straw for me, that was when I knew I had to end things with him, in the hope he would get himself help. The second thing is when you were telling me what you had seen, I knew you were telling the truth. Truth and yourself may be fleeting acquaintances at times, but when I looked into your eyes, I knew you were being honest with me. That photo you saw of us, was one we never posted anywhere. We couldn't, we didn't want to declare our relationship to HR or have them find out in case they made one of us move teams. That photo was the only one we ever had printed off of us together. It was the one they found in his wallet before he jumped. I was so pissed off at him for quitting on himself like that, I tore it up.' Her tears were falling fast now. 'That's why I've been avoiding going in our office. I mean, I've never really believed in ghosts, but this has really freaked me out. What if his spirit is blaming me for what happened? What if it thinks that if I didn't give up on us, he would have found the help he needed instead of giving up on himself?'

'Okay, let's just say ghosts do exist, then I don't think it's you he's after. The threats were made to me and in my home.'

'But that doesn't make any sense. He doesn't even know you.'

'Maybe, he's just trying to protect you, protect this place. There was something you said to me the first time you came to me in my office. Something about how this place was his lifeblood and he wouldn't be responsible for his actions should anyone do anything against it. Perhaps he sees me as a threat to this place with all that I've been doing with my game.'

'Then just quit, Barry. Get out of here. If he wants you out, then just give it to him.'

'But if I quit, that will mean I'm disqualified from playing my game forever.'

'To hell with your stupid game, damn you. If you die, you'll be disqualified from doing **anything** forever.'

McGuire let out a huge sigh.

'I'm scared though.'

'Duh, yeah. You have a vengeful spirit you've managed to piss off coming after you.'

'No. That's not what I mean. I'm scared to stop playing my game. These past few years, this game has been my life. It's defined me. I'm Fire McGuire. For better, or worse, people talk about me. I'm relevant. If I stop, I'll just be, plain old Barry McGuire. This game has brought me joy and purpose, what if I can't find that again in my life? What if I end up burning myself out like Joey, or find myself on a slippery slope like Niles? There has to be more to my life than that.'

Victoria gave him a gentle kiss on the forehead and held his hand.

'Do you want my honest opinion?'

'It's the only opinion that matters, right?'

'Fire McGuire is an asshole. Just being in the same

room as him makes me want to throw blunt, but heavy, objects at him, in the hope it would knock some serious sense into him. Barry McGuire, however. I really like that guy. He's the guy I can talk nonsense with over too much wine. He's the guy who can bring a whole corridor of adults to feel like children again. He's the guy who has so much imagination, drive, and such a different way of looking at the world, he can do things that make him anything but ordinary. More than anything though, Barry McGuire has become my friend.'

McGuire placed his hand on top of Victoria's and gave her a warm smile of gratitude.

Scene Three
The End of the Game

McGuire had returned to his office, via a detour to the nearest church where he had acquired some holy water - just in case Ghost Niles was still pissed off at him.

He left his office door open as he got to work typing on the PC keyboard. He knew that it was vampires that needed to be invited over a threshold, unlike those socially lacking spirits who just seemed to enter into places willy-nilly at their behest. Still, the open door gave him a slight sense of safety.

Though there was still a part of him which believed there had to be some rational explanation, he still wasn't about to take any chances.

He had never typed a resignation letter before. He didn't even know where to start. What to say. All he knew was that he would walk it down to the HR department personally.

It would signal the end of the game for him, and with his friend Victoria's words still fresh in his mind, he felt alright with that.

He began to type.

Dear Sirs,

I would say it is with regret that I type this letter of resignation, but the truth is I do not regret this choice at all.

Sure, I regret that I get to say goodbye to some of the people here, and further regret that I didn't get to know others more.

I regret not staying on to see those I have worked with thrive and become the best versions of themselves. Better versions than I could ever be. But believe me, I will try to be that person elsewhere.

I regret that I will never get to see Sebastian Undergrove again, who despite his ailments still displays an enthusiasm and passion for his fellow humans that inspire those who've been fortunate to meet him.

The reason I don't regret this resignation is, that by doing so, it marks the end of a chapter of my life that I thought defined me. The truth of the matter, however, is that all it ultimately did was control me.

I never gave thought before to the power a sheet of paper holds. A blank page is just that. Nothing more, nothing less. It's a fragile thing. It can be tossed aside and ripped apart with the minimum of effort. Yet with these words now printed upon it, it has become a beacon of hope for me. It has become something strong enough to lift the weight of expectation and burden from my shoulders.

This letter may seem dramatic and excessive to you reading it, but I hope that forces you may not know of and are at unrest also read it and knows the sincerity and repentance in which the words, I quit, have been written.

Yours

Barry McGuire, formerly known as, Fire McGuire.

McGuire stood up to retrieve the page from the printer but was interrupted by a glimpse of a figure walking past the open door of his office. It was Sebastian Undergrove.

'Sebastian,' he called out surprised, yet there was no reply. 'Sebastian,' he called again. 'Wait up.'

By the time McGuire had stepped outside his office, Undergrove was already halfway up the corridor. Gone now was his cane and he was moving quite spritely. Whatever treatment he'd had, McGuire guessed that it had been successful, at least in the short term.

'Sebastian!'

Undergrove turned his head to look at him, smiled his

gentle smile, then carried on walking.

'I need to talk to you about something,' McGuire called out.

His stride turned swift as he attempted to make ground on his boss. He chased him down into the foyer.

Undergrove was already in the elevator. The doors were still open.

'Sebastian, you spritely old bastard. Hold the doors.'

Sebastian still said nothing, he just smiled and pressed the button to go up. McGuire assumed it was to his office.

Whatever game Undergrove was playing with him, he wasn't in the mood for it. Since he was here, he wanted to tell him of his resignation in person, before he handed it to HR. He owed him that much.

He headed to the stairwell and sprinted to the ninth floor. The burning in his legs and lungs mocked him with each step, telling him that perhaps with all that free time he'd had with his days out of work, maybe some time in the gym wouldn't have gone amiss.

He made it to the corridor of the top floor and could see Undergrove ahead. He entered into his office and closed the door behind him.

McGuire allowed himself a few moments to reclaim his breath and composure before knocking.

He had been in such a rush over trying to catch up with Undergrove, he hadn't even fully considered what it was he would even say to him - outside of the fact he was quitting the company with immediate effect.

Despite many of the situations he had found himself in whilst playing the game, he had always been fearless and unashamed over his antics, and the lengths he would often go to. Yet, for once, he was feeling embarrassed. Embarrassed over how foolish he would sound if pushed to tell the truth behind his reasons for quitting.

'Well, the reason I'm quitting is because I have a vengeful spirit of one of your ex-employees out to get me, and unless I change the errors of my ways, I'll likely be dead by the end of the day.'

Upon reflection, this wasn't even the most ridiculous thing that had come out of his mouth over the past few years. Yet, they say the truth is often stranger than fiction.

Another truth was that McGuire was also as worried about Undergrove's feelings towards hearing the news as he was his own at delivering it.

For whatever reason, Undergrove had taken a real shine and connection to him. He was worried that he would see McGuire's leaving, especially with such a nonsensical excuse, as a personal smite. The poor bastard was going through enough physical hardships as it was, without having to endure emotional setbacks too.

McGuire's hand lingered by the panel of the office door but was thwarted from making its connection to the wood by the sound of a telephone ringing from inside the office.

The telephone was being left to ring.

A part of McGuire hoped that Undergrove simply just didn't want to pick it up. He was already acting in a weird mood. Yet a terrible feeling inside of him couldn't help but feel that the reasons for him not answering were cause for alarm.

Undergrove hadn't even answered the calls out to him in the corridor, all he could do was smile at him. Maybe he knew that his time was up, and he wanted to face his curtain call with a defiant shit-eating smile rather than a look of defeat.

McGuire abstained from knocking, and instead opted to burst into the office uninvited.

He was fully prepared to be met with the unwelcome sight of Undergrove catatonic or worse, hunched over his desk. Yet, the scene that greeted him, to his surprise, was that no one was in the office at all.

'How could that be?' he thought. He had followed Undergrove to his office, he had watched him go in. There was no way he could have left so quickly without him not noticing.

Then a worse thought entered his mind. Perhaps he left his office a different way.

His eyes quickly turned towards the windows. Had that poor bastard really jumped? Deciding the fate of his inevitable death on his own terms.

No. It couldn't be that. All the windows were closed and intact.

The phone still rang.

A befuddled McGuire picked it up to answer.

'I'm sorry, Mr Undergrove isn't here right now,' he spoke.

The voice the other end of the line seemed taken aback by this statement.

'Yes, I know. Sebastian Undergrove passed away two nights ago. I'm the solicitor for his estate. My name's, Windsor Hemlow, from Hemlow and Partners. I'm just calling through on this number Mr Undergrove listed as his contact number to start making the funeral arrangements and the reading of the will.'

'There's got to be some mistake,' McGuire defied. 'I literally saw him a few minutes ago.'

'I wish that was true, sir, believe me. Mr Undergrove was a dear man, but alas, I signed the certificate of death myself. Is there another number I can perhaps call? I seem to recall him mentioning Misters Singer and Hensley, who he indicated were aware of what his funeral plans would be.'

'Um, er, I'll get them to call you back.' His voice was languid in its response.

McGuire placed the phone back on the receiver. A cavalry of thoughts charged his mind, none of them coherent.

'What's up, Barry?' A familiar voice came from behind him. 'It looks like you've seen a ghost.'

He turned around and saw Sebastian Undergrove standing in the doorway.

'Are you?'

Undergrove smiled a gentle and sympathetic smile. 'No, Barry. I'm far, far, worse.'

McGuire could only watch on aghast as the figure standing in front of him changed in an instant to another. It was the investor, Solomon Wright.

'I think you better take a seat,' Solomon suggested in a tone that was more of an order.

McGuire begrudgingly obliged. Not because he wanted to obey this person in front of him, whoever or whatever it was, but because he could feel all strength vacating him.

'May I just say,' Solomon continued. 'I've been a big fan of your work for a few years now. Ever since you started playing your little game. So, when the opportunity came to be a part of it, I jumped at the chance to play this final round with you. Take it for what it's worth, but that's the highest compliment I can give a person, especially considering how busy I am with my own job.'

'Are you the devil?' McGuire asked coyly.

'Well, technically, no. I mean, I'm not "*the*" Devil. That old asshole retired a long time ago. The last I heard; he was living it up large at some villa in Florida. I am however, how shall we say it? A regional manager of Hell.

To break it down in business terms, back in the olden days, when the population was still manageable, Hell was just a start-up company. Yet, as humankind grew, so did supply and demand for our services. We very quickly became a hugely successful global franchise, kind of like Starbucks, if you will. Come to think of it, that is one of ours too.'

'But why me?'

'Well, you were never told the truth about your real father.' Solomon adopted a mock Darth Vader voice. 'I am your father.'

He watched the shock appear on McGuire's face and let out a mischievous little chuckle.

'Nah, I'm just messing with you. That gag never gets

old. The fact of the matter, why you, is that you're one of the worst kinds of sinners. Granted, you're not a murderer or a sex offender, or any of that malarky. But you've been committing the sin of wasted potential for the last few years. Okay, I admit, it may not be one of the flashier sounding Seven Deadly Sins. If anything, you could say it's more of a case of being one of the Seven Slightly Hazardous Sins.

The bottom line is, you've got all the potential and ability in the world, Barry. You have a wonderful imagination, common sense, intelligence, personality. You could have been anything you wanted to be. Yet, you insisted on playing that game of yours instead. You were so proud of that ridiculous Fallow Formula, that you became blinded by it. You failed to see what good is all the extra time in your life if you choose to do nothing with it. You have no friends, no family, no special person to share it with. Even when you finally made a true connection with someone such as Victoria, who could have brought you so much happiness with your friendship, you were still more focussed on playing your game.'

'But I'm not dead yet. She's helped me see the error of my ways. I know I can be better just by being me. I'm going to change. You have no right to my soul.'

'This isn't some Christmas Carol kind of story, and, quite frankly, you're more of an Ebeneezer Stooge than an Ebeneezer Scrooge. Just because you've realised you've been an asshole; it doesn't automatically make you a better person. It just makes you someone who knows he's an asshole.

You're not going to get any second chances to better yourself, and I already have claim to you. You signed your services over to me on your first day here.'

Solomon produced the contract from inside his jacket and handed it over to McGuire.

'Does this look familiar to you?'

It did.

'But I read through that contract carefully,' McGuire protested. 'There is no mention in the small print of selling my soul to anyone, let alone you. I'm always extra careful to read the small print.'

Solomon just smiled and shook his head.

'That's the problem with people these days. You're so focussed on being caught out by the little things; you don't seem to pay attention to the bigger picture.'

McGuire gave the document another read through, and he saw it. Plain as day. His contract of employment wasn't to Play Dates Ltd, but to Sebastian Undergrove and any creditors.

'He's dead though,' McGuire spoke unevenly, already knowing that this would be a triviality that Solomon had thought of.

'Death is just an inconvenience rather than an inevitability. Sebastian Undergrove signed his soul over to me several months ago, which makes me his creditor. I've got to tell you, getting someone as righteous and as good-hearted as Undergrove on my books is a real coup de grâce.

In my line of work, one righteous soul is worth a thousand sinners.

All it took was the promise for Play Dates to return to its former glory once he had passed. The way he saw it, his eternity of damnation was worth the sacrifice of continuing to bring joy and happiness to millions of children around the world. You have no idea how much he was against the idea of hiring a train wreck such as yourself to his beloved company when he had received your application, and it took a lot of convincing from me for him to take you on. When I told him you were already damned anyway, and if it wasn't going to be at Play Dates, it would only be somewhere else, he eventually yielded. It's true what Jaycon said of him. He wanted the guilt of an employees' death to be his and no one else's.'

For someone as astute as yourself, I'm amazed you

didn't figure out something was amiss earlier. You were just so wrapped up in your world and your game. Victoria even said to you the odds of you hiring Jerry's long-lost daughter were more than a million to one, yet you still wouldn't have it.'

McGuire watched as Solomon changed appearance again, this time to that of Candy Cane.

'I'm going to let you into a little secret,' she spoke. 'Candy isn't my real name.'

'You twisted bastard,' McGuire yelled. 'Poor Jerry will be heartbroken.'

'Stop acting like you care about his feelings, Barry. Besides, it's all part of the bigger game. I'm sure you will appreciate that. Good old Jerry, he'll be devastated when Cynthia disappears again. So much so that he'll even be prepared to sell his soul to me so that they could all live happily as a family again for the rest of their living days. Of course, I'll be more than happy to oblige him. It's as I said, one righteous soul is worth that of a thousand.'

'What about Victoria? Please tell me she'll be kept out of this. If you go near her, I'll kill you, I swear.'

'Have no fear, her shining white knight. She truly is the one that got away, for both of us. Undergrove has seen that she is set on a greater path and, alas, safe from my net. The reading of his last will and testament is going to reveal that he is leaving Play Dates to Victoria.

Her performance at the pitch, and her insistence that she would put any products that would aid the disadvantaged over any profit was enough of a swayer for him to know that the company would be in the right hands.

But of course, Sebastian wasn't the only one looking out for her.'

McGuire watched as Solomon morphed again. This time into the figure of Niles.

'Niles' failure and path to despair was all a part of my game, there are no accidents in this life. Everything is interconnected. Niles' product tanked because the director of a rival toy company made a deal with me to see his competition fail. Niles' downfall set him on a path that would see him hit rock bottom, and when you hit rock bottom, you either find God or the devil at the end of a bottle. He chose me.

We made a deal before his death, that Victoria would live a fulfilled and successful life after he had passed. As a fiend of my word, I'm going to see to it that her products will go on to be very successful and change a great many deal of lives for the better. She will get a call tomorrow from one of the investors with a sudden change of heart, and a desire to invest heavily in her product as it was originally designed and intended.'

The figure switched back to that of Solomon.

'So, what happens to me?' McGuire asked. 'His voice was broken and weak.

'As per our contract, you work for me now. I've got a perfect job for you in admin. Don't worry about your Fallow Formula though. There's no such thing as 9-5 where we're going.'

Solomon gestured for McGuire to come with him. McGuire resisted.

'Now now Barry. No one likes a sore loser. If you don't play nice, believe me when I say, things will get a lot worse for you.'

Solomon snapped his fingers and McGuire could feel his flesh starting to rot and itch. It had been just like Joeys in the nightmare he'd had.

'Your brother tried resisting too. It didn't end well for him. All he wanted was for you to get a job for life. Well, you're about to start it.'

The tears flowing down McGuire's face stung at the exposed wounds on his cheeks, yet it was the words that Solomon spoke that caused him the most despair.

Solomon clicked his fingers. McGuire's face was back to normal.

'That is just a verbal warning to you. Believe me, you do not want a disciplinary for not listening to your new boss where we're going. So, am I going to have to ask you again?'

Barry shook his head, feebly. He was broken now.

He followed Solomon down the corridor towards the foyer and the left-hand elevator.

The doors opened. The Play Dates song was playing again, only this time it was slower, more sinister. The voices singing were mocking him.

'Going down?' Solomon taunted.

The elevator's descent seemed to last more than an hour, yet still it moved downwards.

Then, an idea came to McGuire, followed by a hefty and sincere laugh.

As he continued to chuckle, he could see the look of intrigue, almost discomfort, on Solomon's face.

'May I ask what is amusing you?'

Barry said nothing at first. Yet, his mind was filled with a sudden excitement - optimism even.

He had yet to hand his notice in for his position at Play Dates. As such, by the rules of the game, he was still very much eligible to play, and play he would. It was going to be the ultimate round.

Sure, getting sacked from hell was going to be a tall ask, and it would take every trick and tactic in his playbook. But if anyone could win this game it would be him.

He was Fire McGuire after all.

The End

ABOUT THE AUTHOR

Steve McElhenny is Welsh, short, and hairy.

Also available from the author.

Draculand
Lethal Dangerousness
Lethal Forcefulness
The Man Who Thought He Was a Cat
The Girl with a Porcelain Face
Kingshire Falls
Avenging Aranis: Episode One – The Flames of the Inferno

Printed in Great Britain
by Amazon

a11a1a45-7bfe-4ffa-9ed5-de2f09d76f47R01